I wanted to disappear.

Immediately.

Why did I always look my absolute *worst* when I crossed paths with Kyle?

Why couldn't he have found me a few hours earlier when I was looking like a burst of sunshine? Now I looked like I'd been caught in a hurricane. I'd lost an earring, my hair was a mess, and I squished when I walked. Kyle, on the other hand, in his khakis, blue-and-white striped polo shirt, baseball jacket, and docksiders, looked like he'd stepped out of the pages of an Abercrombie & Fitch catalog.

"Kyle!" My teeth were starting to chatter. "W-w-what are you doing here?"

XOXOXOX(

Read all the FIRST KISSES books:

Trust Me by Rachel Hawthorne

The Boyfriend Trick by Stephie Davis

Puppy Love by Jenny Collins

It Had to Be You by Sabrina Jordan

FIRST KISSES

It Had to Be You

Sabrina Jordan

HARPER TEEN

An Imprint of HarperCollins*Publishers*

HarperTeen is an imprint of
HarperCollins Publishers.

www.harperteen.com

Library of Congress Catalog Card Number:
2006934341
ISBN-10: 0-06-114313-8
ISBN-13: 978-0-06-114313-7

Typography by Andrea Vandergrift
❖
First HarperTeen edition, 2007

This novel is for three very special teachers:

Mrs. Susan Scroppo, who in fifth grade asked me, after reading a short story I'd written, "Are you going to be a writer when you grow up?"

and

Miss Loretta Ali and Mrs. Joan Porcaro, my sixth grade teachers, who always encouraged me and always had nice things to say about my writing.

It Had
to Be You

Chapter One

XOXOX

I am a girly-girl.

With three older brothers who are obsessed with sports and cars and video games, it would have been easy for me to grow up a tomboy, but I didn't.

From the time I was little, I've loved being a girl! Dresses with ruffles. Colored tights. Shiny black Mary Janes. I used to wear them all! Very rarely would I wear T-shirts and jeans, but if I did, there was always something feminine about them. Like my jeans wouldn't be blue. They'd be yellow or purple and trimmed with lace on the cuffs. And my T-shirts would say things like: DADDY'S LITTLE GIRL or SWEET AS SUGAR.

I used to have tea parties with my stuffed animals and I would serve cakes made with my Easy-Bake oven. Cliché, I know. I even had every Barbie imaginable, including all the accessories, as well as a few Bratz dolls. Confession: I always loved my Barbies more than my Bratz dolls. Barbie just seemed more elegant. And she had her own Dream House!

I've always had pierced ears. My oldest brother, Rob, who's nineteen and just finished his first year of college, says this is because when I was a baby and our mom used to take me out in my carriage, people would always stop her and say, "What a cute baby boy!" even though I was wearing pink and I had a Pebbles Flintstone hairstyle (a tuft of hair sticking up on the top of my head and tied with a bright-colored ribbon).

Earrings are fun. My jewelry box is filled with all sorts of different styles. Some days I like wearing tiny hoops. Other days I like wearing earrings that are long and dangling. Sometimes I'll just go simple and wear gold studs. My mom has a fabulous earring collection and sometimes she'll let me borrow a pair, but *only* if I ask permission. Sneaking into her jewelry box is *not* allowed. That's because her earrings are made of real gold and silver and diamonds while mine are all pretty much costume jewelry.

When I was little, my mom used to braid my hair in pigtails. Some days she'd give me a ponytail. But whatever hairstyle she gave me, she always used silk ribbons and cute barrettes and hair clips. My hair is still long and I love styling it in different ways. No short-and-sassy hairstyle for me! My hair reaches past my shoulders to the middle of my back and the color is chestnut brown, although sometimes, like during the summer, if I'm out in the sun for a long time, highlights will appear. My best friend, Caitlyn, is always telling me she would kill to have my hair. I don't know what she's complaining about. Her hair is super curly and a gorgeous red color. Not carrot red but a rich auburn. Like in shampoo ads in magazines. But she hates the color and is always trying to straighten the curls out of her hair.

Caitlyn and I have been best friends since kindergarten. On the first day of school, we both brought our Cabbage Patch Kids to school for show-and-tell. The dolls were identical and we decided that they were long-lost sisters and it was up to us to make sure they stayed in touch.

Caitlyn practically lives at my house and when we're not hanging out together, we're either on the phone or instant messaging when we're online. We tell each other *everything* although there's a secret I've been keeping from her.

It's not that I don't want to tell her my secret, but I can't. I've been told that part of the job I've just taken is keeping my identity a secret.

I know this all sounds mysterious and confusing, but it really isn't. And there's a perfectly logical explanation.

This September I'll be a freshman at North Marshall High School and I've been picked to inherit the job of being the anonymous freshman advice columnist, Dear Daisy, for the high school's website. Daisy has been around *forever*. I think she was even giving out advice when my parents were both freshmen there! Before websites existed, she had her own column in the school's newspaper. Every year a new freshman takes over as Daisy, writing the column and dispensing advice.

Working on my junior high's newspaper, writing and editing articles, is what got me the job of Dear Daisy. I know the importance of extracurricular activities. Colleges look for that kind of stuff in addition to good grades, so it's never too early to start participating.

My guidance counselor, who I met when I went to pick up my class schedule in June, was the one who told me about the Dear Daisy position. He thought I would be good at it, but he also told me that there were five other girls who were just as qualified as I was to take over the column. If I was interested in becoming

Dear Daisy, then I'd have to submit a sample column and after all the columns were compared, a decision would be made.

Naturally, I was interested. Who wouldn't want their own column? Although I'd be behind the scenes dispensing advice, it would still be a huge responsibility. So I went home with the questions, answered them the best that I could, and sent them back. A week later my guidance counselor called to tell me I was this year's Dear Daisy!

"Now remember, Emma," he reminded me as we were finishing up our call. "Other than your family, no one is to know you're Dear Daisy. This rule must be followed."

"No one?" I had asked. "Not even my best friend?"

"No one. If people knew the identity of Dear Daisy they might be uncomfortable or self-conscious coming to her for advice that can be personal. At all times we have to be sensitive to their privacy and yours."

"That makes sense." The last thing I wanted was to embarrass a fellow classmate. I was also told that there would be a teacher who would approve all my responses before they got posted.

So Caitlyn didn't know that I was Daisy. I'm sure if she did, she'd be very happy for me.

As for my family . . .

Well, my parents were excited, but then they're always excited when my brothers and I do well at school. They both gave me congratulatory hugs and kisses, and my mom and I baked a cake in the shape of a giant daisy.

My brothers were another story.

Rob, Michael, and Aaron didn't say anything when they heard my news but that's not unusual for them. All they did was ask Mom if the daisy cake we'd made was chocolate on the inside (it was) and if they could each have two pieces. I wanted to scream! I'm not a sports buff—I'll admit that—but they are my brothers and even though they drive me crazy I want them to know that I care for them. So sometimes I'll go and watch one of their stupid basketball or baseball or hockey games and pretend to be interested even though I'm bored out of my mind. They couldn't give me a "Way to go, Emma!" or even a "Congrats!" Argh! I wanted to mash their faces into the cake that Mom was handing out!

They did agree, though, to keep my secret and not breathe a word to anyone that I was going to be Dear Daisy. I believe them. My brothers might torture me at home, but when it comes to the outside world, they can be very protective. I don't understand why they can't be like that all the time!

I'm extremely proud of the fact that I've been chosen to be Dear Daisy because if there's one thing I know how to do, it's give out advice.

I'm always cool, calm, and collected. I never let my emotions get the best of me (and with the way my brothers drive me crazy, that's saying a lot). I'm always organized and on top of things. Deadlines matter to me.

Most important, when it comes to advice and guidance, my girlfriends always come to me first.

Last fall my friend Gwen asked me how to get the attention of a guy she had a crush on.

My advice? Just tell him!

The next day Gwen called to tell me that my advice had worked!

My answers are always short and to the point. Why beat around the bush? If you like a guy, but he doesn't like you, isn't it better to know sooner rather than later?

Still, it never hurts to be prepared, which was why I had checked out a bunch of relationship books from the local library: *It's Not You, It's Me, Why Doesn't He Like Me?, How to Get the Man of Your Dreams in Thirty Days or Less, Man Trouble: Is He Really Worth It?*

I'm always this way when it comes to projects. First I make a list and write down what my objective is. Next I decide what research materials I'm going to need and then I gather the materials I need to make my project happen. I like to be prepared so I can do the best job possible.

Last year I decided to take a cooking class on the weekends. I've always loved the Food Channel but there's a difference between watching them make an elaborate meal on TV and then trying to do it yourself in your own kitchen. Trust me, I've tried! Disaster! So I figured if I did want to learn how to cook, I should learn from an expert and not try to do it myself.

The class I signed up for was every Saturday and Sunday afternoon for three hours and taught by a local chef. We learned how to make everything! But I didn't just limit myself to Chef Unger's lessons. When I throw myself into a project, I want to give it my best shot. Not 100 percent but 110 percent. I got subscriptions to all the top food magazines. I read lots of cookbooks and I kept practicing in our kitchen. My mom and dad were always great at critiquing my dishes, telling me what they liked and didn't like. My brothers? Please! They would suspiciously sniff every dish I made and then claim not to be hungry. Those three are walking stomachs. They're *always* hungry. If they did eat something I made, they would claim that it tasted awful, which was *not* the case. They live to torture me!

In the beginning I stuck with recipes from cookbooks, but now I'm starting to become a little daring and try my own recipes. I'm not saying every dish I make is a mouthwatering success, but it's fun to experiment.

Anyway, it was the end of July and I was in my bedroom, giving myself a day of beauty while I was flipping through the relationship books and taking notes. That night Caitlyn and I would be going to the movies and it never hurts to look one's best! Even though a lot of the guys in my class had gone away for the summer, there were always a few that remained in town. And you never know when you might run into one of them.

The first rule of a day of beauty is that I'm allowed to look my worst. If I'm going to be slathering my hair and face and nails with all sorts of creams and lotions and oils, I don't want to ruin my clothes. Usually I'll wear my rattiest pair of jeans and an old T-shirt that I've swiped from one of my brothers. Today I was in a pair of cutoff jean shorts and Aaron's VOTE FOR PEDRO T-shirt from the movie *Napoleon Dynamite*.

I always start my day of beauty by shampooing and conditioning my hair with my favorite products. I *swear* by Garnier. Then after I've rinsed my hair, I add an extra-deep conditioner—Pantene this time—and wrap my hair in a towel, turban-style, for forty-five minutes. Then I move on to my face, applying a blue mud pack. This isn't one of those masks that's thin and elasticky, like chewing gum. It's the kind that dries in layers so there's a thick mask on your face.

While my hair is conditioning and my mud pack is solidifying, I move on to my toes. First, I insert wads of cotton between my toes. Then I strip my toes of my old polish with nail polish remover, dry them, and paint them with a new coat of color. Because it's summer, I had decided on a color called Pink Lemonade. It looked pretty in the bottle, so I was hoping it would look pretty on my toes. Colors can sometimes be deceiving—what looks good in the bottle doesn't always look good on your nails. Caitlyn and I learned this lesson the hard way last fall. We'd bought a color called Passionate Plum. In the bottle it looked all nice and purply. But after it got on our nails? Yikes! Once the color had dried, it looked like we had painted our nails black! We'd instantly taken the polish off, but not before Aaron got a peek at it. For weeks he kept calling us Goth Girls and asking us where our coven was.

What I liked about the brand I was using today—Revlon Nail Enamel—was that after the polish had dried, it still had that "wet" look.

I had just finished polishing my toenails and was buffing my fingernails with an emery board when the doorbell rang. Being that I was in my bedroom on the second floor and all three of my brothers were on the first floor, I ignored it, thinking that one of them would answer it.

Ha!

They didn't.

And so the doorbell rang again.

And again.

And again.

Both my parents were at work, so unless I said something, that doorbell was going to keep ringing and ringing.

"Will someone please answer that?" I called

out as sweetly as possible. After fourteen years of growing up with my brothers, I knew if I sounded angry or upset, I wouldn't get them to do anything.

Total silence.

No one answered me.

And the doorbell rang again.

I tried hard to ignore the ringing but it was driving me crazy. The three of them were downstairs in the family room, watching a movie, and I was one floor above them. They were closer to the front door than me!

And what was with the person constantly ringing the doorbell? Why hadn't they given up and left? What was so important that they had to keep ringing our doorbell?

The doorbell rang for the sixth time — I was keeping count! — only this time the ring seemed longer and sharper.

Was the person now keeping their finger on the bell before letting go instead of just giving a quick press?

It was probably a salesman. I guess he or

she could tell we were home because my brothers had the TV on in the front room.

I vowed that I was absolutely, positively *not* going to answer the front door but when the bell rang *again*, I couldn't stand it anymore.

I got off my bed and hopped into the hallway, trying not to smudge my toenails. But Aaron had left his skateboard in front of my room and I almost slipped on it. While I stumbled and tried to catch my balance, my perfectly polished toes—which were still wet!—dragged against the floor, getting all smudgy. I'd have to redo them. Not to mention clean the polish off the floor before Mom came home from work!

Since I didn't have to worry about my toenails any longer, I stomped down the front stairs just as the doorbell started ringing again. By this point, I was beyond angry. Whoever was standing on the other side of the door was going to get a piece of my mind.

A big piece!

I flung open the front door.

"What is it?!" I snarled. "Whatever you're selling, we're not interested so you can just go! Just . . ."

The rest of the words died in my throat.

Instead of the pushy salesman I'd been expecting to find waiting on our doorstep, there was a guy my own age standing in front of me.

Correction: a *very cute* guy.

I started to smile until I realized I couldn't. My mouth wouldn't move. It was frozen in place.

And then I remembered.

The mud pack!

Yikes!

My hands flew to my face and then to the turban on my head.

Suddenly I remembered the way I looked.

The way I was dressed.

I was a walking disaster!

I was the Before girl in all those Before-and-After ads you saw in magazines and on TV.

On the other hand, the guy standing across from me was cute, cute, *cute*! He had sky blue eyes and wheat-colored blond hair that he wore in a summer crew cut that was just starting to grow out. He was wearing a bright blue tank top, white surfer shorts, and sandals. I couldn't help but notice his feet. Unlike my brothers', his toenails were buff and shiny and not grody with dirt!

After staring at each other in silence, he finally stuttered, "Um, does your bell not work?"

"What?"

"I—I—um—never mind," he said somewhat warily, like he wasn't sure if he should stand in place or try to make a run for it.

Then he held a pie plate out to me. Actually, he stretched his arm out as far as it would go without actually moving forward.

Like he was afraid of touching me!

The nerve!

He was acting like I had cooties. Or that I was germy!

I snatched the plate out of his hands. As I did, I got a closer look at it, noticing the pattern.

17

"This is our pie plate," I said. "Where did you get it?"

"Your, um, mom sent it over yesterday with a blueberry pie. My family just moved into the house next door."

"The house next door?"

The lightbulb went on over my head.

The house next door!

For years the old Victorian house next door had been empty. But earlier this spring it had been sold and renovations had been going on. According to the neighborhood gossip vine, a new family would be moving to the block.

Apparently, they already had.

This cutie was my new next-door neighbor and here I was looking like the Bride of Frankenstein!

"I'm Emma Miller," I said, trying to sound sweet and friendly. I needed to do some damage control! "I wasn't home yesterday when you moved in, otherwise I would have come over to say hello. Welcome to the neighborhood."

Cute Guy gave me a look like he wasn't sure if he wanted to stay in the neighborhood.

"What's your name?" I asked.

"Kyle. Kyle O'Reilly."

"Nice to meet you, Kyle. Would you like to come in?" I held the front door open wider. "My brothers are in the family room watching a movie."

Kyle pointed behind his back with his thumb, stating to walk backward. As though he was afraid to turn his back on me! Who did he think I was? Medusa? Was Medusa the one you weren't supposed to turn your back on otherwise you'd turn to stone, or was it some other Greek goddess?

"Maybe another time. I've got to get home," he said. "We've still got a lot of unpacking to do."

"Okay," I said. "Maybe I'll see you around?"

If he could have run backward, he would have.

"Maybe," he said.

"Okay," I said, giving him a wave. "Bye."

I closed the front door just as Michael came out of the family room with an empty bowl of popcorn.

"What's with the getup, Em? Early Halloween costume? What are you supposed to be? A zombie?"

My second-oldest brother instantly realized he'd said the *wrong* thing as I opened my mouth and screamed, "You guys are *so* dead!" and raced back to my bedroom.

Chapter Two

XOXOX

always dress to impress.

Clothes matter.

Clothes are important.

At least they are to me!

I don't understand people who dress like slobs. Do they not look at themselves in the mirror before they leave their homes? And I'm not just talking about guys. Some of the girls I go to school with? *Brrr!* Their outfits give me nightmares. I'm not trying to be mean, it's just that what you wear says something about who you are, so you should always pay attention to how you dress. In my opinion, anyway.

I will admit that I did *not* look my best when I first met Kyle. Okay, okay, I looked like such a fashion mess I would have probably caused Miranda Priestly, the evil boss from *The Devil Wears Prada*, to go blind. But that wouldn't be the case the next time I saw him.

After warning my brothers that the next time the doorbell rang, I would *not* be answering it—of course, they ignored me, as they usually do, which made me only madder—I'd gone back upstairs to my bedroom. My relaxing day of beauty was over, so I scrubbed my face clean and then washed out my hair and blow-dried it before deciding I needed to do something fun.

Which was why I was standing in front of my closet, trying to figure out what I was going to wear to the movies that night with Caitlyn.

I have always loved clothes and I'm in awe of designers who can take bolts of fabric and turn them into wearable pieces of art.

I always watch the MTV Music Awards, the MTV Video Awards, the VH-1 Awards, the Grammys, the Oscars, and any other awards show that I can find. I'm hooked on seeing what the celebrities are wearing.

I have subscriptions to *Vogue*, *Elle*, and *Cosmo Girl*, as well as *People*, *US Weekly*, *Entertainment Weekly*, and *In Touch*. The pages of these magazines are always filled with celebrities wearing designer outfits. And I live for the Best Dressed/Worst Dressed issues.

My brothers think I'm crazy, but what can you expect from three guys who think "dressing up" is wearing socks with their loafers and tucking in their shirts? Oh, and combing their hair! Rob's gotten a little bit better since he started college—he combs his hair more often but I think that's because he now has a semi-serious girlfriend, Cathy, who he's been dating for almost a year and she makes him—but Michael and Aaron are still slobs.

As much as I hate to admit this, my brothers are all kind of hotties, despite their slobbiness. They all have brown hair and brown eyes, but they don't look identical. Each has his own style to match his interests.

Rob's the jock of the family. In high school

he was the captain of the football and basketball teams. He also played tennis and ran track. He's like six foot one and has broad shoulders. Rob mostly wears khakis and bright-colored polo shirts.

Michael, on the other hand, is very laid back. He's seventeen, loves music, and is always walking around with his iPod. He lives in baggy jeans and T-shirts. He collects vintage tees and some of his T-shirts go all the way back to the sixties and seventies when groups like The Doors and Led Zeppelin were big. His hair is way longer than Rob's or Aaron's and he wears it in a ponytail most days. He's not as tall as Rob, just a little under six feet, but Dad keeps saying he's going to catch up.

Aaron, who's fifteen, is a combination of Rob and Michael, but much shorter (right now he's just five foot seven). His biggest fear is that he's going to stop growing, but Dad keeps telling him he's going to be just as tall as Rob someday. He's not a jock at school, but he'll watch any sports event on TV. He likes music, but he's more into video games. Then again, they all like video games—they're boys! When it comes to dressing, he really doesn't have a personal style. Usually he'll just wear jeans and a plaid shirt thrown over a T-shirt. I think he's still trying to figure himself out. Or maybe he just doesn't care what he looks like!

Everyone assumes because I'm a girl and I'm the baby of the family that I have the biggest bedroom in our house, but I don't. Rob, being the oldest, has the biggest bedroom. It used to be the attic but it was converted into a bedroom. Very *Brady Bunch*—I know! Michael and Aaron have the second-biggest bedroom because they share.

I have the smallest bedroom.

Which means I have the smallest closet.

But it's filled with the most clothes!

My closet is a work of art. I don't have just one rack to hang my clothes from, I have two, one on top of the other. Boxes of shoes line the floor of my closet and on the inside of the two doors, I have hooks for hangers. Besides my closet, I also have a dresser and a trunk at the foot of my bed to store my clothes.

I surveyed the interior of my closet and began flipping through the hangers.

Some of my clothes I love and I will wear them over and over again.

Other outfits cause me to shake my head and ask myself, *What was I thinking?! Why did I buy that?*

Decisions, decisions.

I needed something comfy and casual to wear tonight.

Cute but chic.

Finally, I decided on a raspberry-colored skirt decorated with tiny white polka dots, a short-sleeved white cotton shirt with pink buttons at the top, and sandals to show off my Pink Lemonade toes (I'd repaired the damage after blow-drying my hair and the finished results were fab!). My jewelry would be minimal—just a charm bracelet on one wrist and my watch on the other—and I would wear my hair loose.

I peeked outside my bedroom window at the house next door, hoping to get a glimpse of Kyle, but I didn't see him. Rats! But maybe he'd be around tonight when I left to go to the movies and he'd do a double-take, wondering who the cute girl leaving my house was.

That thought put a smile on my face.

I didn't have a smile on my face when I met Caitlyn for the movie.

Kyle hadn't seen me leave the house, so as far as he was concerned, I was still the She-Beast Who Lived Next Door.

"Why so glum?" Caitlyn asked, giving me a hug as we walked up to the ticket window.

"You will *not* believe what happened to me today!"

As we waited in line to buy our tickets, I filled Caitlyn in on my encounter with Kyle. When I finished, I expected Caitlyn to start asking me questions.

Well, she asked me a question, but it wasn't the one I was expecting.

"Was Aaron at home?"

I sighed. Caitlyn's latest crush is my brother Aaron. Since he's only a year older than us, he's always played the part of Annoying Older

Brother, more so than Rob and Michael. I think it's because we're so close in age. When I was little, and Caitlyn used to come over to play with me, Aaron would snatch away our jacks or hide our jump ropes. He'd kidnap our dolls and hold them for ransom. When Caitlyn and I would have sleepovers, he'd never let us watch what we wanted on TV. Then he'd try to scare us in the middle of the night by pretending to be the boogeyman. (Caitlyn used to be afraid of the dark, so whenever she slept over, my mom kept a night-light on in my room. One time, Aaron hid under my bed and when we fell asleep, he turned off the night-light and then started moaning under my bed. Eventually Caitlyn woke up, saw the room was pitch-black, and heard the moans coming from under my bed. What really pushed her over the edge, though, and caused her to start screaming was when Aaron—in a disguised voice—said, "I'm sooo hungry. I think I'm going to eat a little girl named Caitlyn." It took almost an hour for my parents to calm Caitlyn down. As for Aaron, his television privileges were taken away for a week.) At Halloween he'd steal our trick-or-treat bags and eat all the good candy bars like our Snickers and Mounds and leave only the crappy candy behind.

Caitlyn has forgotten all that. It's like she has amnesia. All of a sudden, she thinks Aaron is cute and wants to know if he thinks she's cute, too.

I've told Caitlyn that I'm not playing messenger. If she's interested in Aaron, she should just tell him, but so far she's refused to follow my advice.

Instead, she acts like a giggling airhead whenever she's over at my house and Aaron is in the same room with us. It's starting to get annoying, and Aaron is so clueless. I don't know how much longer I can take it.

"Yes, Aaron was at home."

"Did he ask about me?"

"Why would he ask about you?"

This is a new thing with Caitlyn. She's always asking me if Aaron has asked about her.

She shrugged. "I don't know. But did he?"

"No, he didn't," I said, wanting to get back

to my story about Kyle.

"Oh."

Caitlyn looked so bummed that I decided to cheer her up. "You haven't been over in a couple of days. Maybe that's why he didn't ask."

Caitlyn instantly smiled. "That's right! I'll have to come over this week."

After we got our tickets, we walked into the movie theater. The cool air-conditioning felt delicious after the sticky humidity outside.

"Want to go to Jones Beach tomorrow?" Caitlyn asked as we found two seats in the middle of the theater. "My sister is going with her girlfriends. They could take us."

Caitlyn and I live on Long Island, outside of New York City. Jones Beach is *the* beach to go to, especially at night when they have all sorts of concerts. I haven't been to a concert yet but my brothers have.

"That sounds like fun."

"Make sure you wear your yellow one-piece."

"Why?"

"So when you're leaving the house, your next-door neighbor can see how great you look in it!"

"I looked great tonight and he didn't see me. What makes you think he'll see me tomorrow morning?"

"Good point." Caitlyn was silent for a moment. "You know," she said—somewhat perkily, I thought—"this situation will actually work to your advantage."

"How?" I asked.

"Well, you looked pretty horrible, right?"

"Don't remind me," I groaned, remembering the look of stunned horror on Kyle's face.

"The next time he sees you, you're going to look gorgeous! You'll be the complete opposite of what he remembers. Oooh! Wait, wait, wait!" Caitlyn clapped her hands excitedly. "I just came up with a brilliant idea. Why leave things to chance? Make yourself as gorgeous as possible and then *you* ring *his* doorbell!"

It's not often that I'm at a loss for words, but Caitlyn's idea left me speechless. Why hadn't I thought of it? It was the exact same kind of advice I would have given.

"That could definitely work," I said. "But what will I wear?"

"Hello!" Caitlyn exclaimed. "Don't tell me you've forgotten the huge sale at H.O.F.—it's in two days!"

H.O.F.—House of Fashion—was my favorite store at the mall. They had semi-designer brand names, as well as quality knockoffs at reasonable prices. Twice a year they had a big sale, marking down merchandise by as much as 75 percent, and this week would be their big summer clearance sale. I had been saving every penny I could get my hands on—babysitting money, birthday money, graduation money—for the big day. After all, I was going to be a freshman in September and I needed to supplement my wardrobe with some new purchases.

"We'll get you an outfit that will make Kyle stop in his tracks. And not from fright!"

"Sounds like a plan!"

"So is this movie supposed to be any good?"

Caitlyn whispered as the lights started to dim and the previews began.

"I don't know," I answered. "But it stars Lindsay Lohan."

Caitlyn rolled her eyes. "Ugh! Lindsay Lohan!"

"Jealous much?" I teased.

"You know it," Caitlyn sighed. "The biggest movie star to ever come out of Long Island! Why can't I be like her?"

"Why can't we all?"

"All she has to do is wiggle her pinkie and all the guys come running," Caitlyn said. "So what's the plot of this movie?"

"Lindsay's an heiress but she doesn't know it. Her grandfather disinherited her mother or something. Now her grandfather is dying and he doesn't have anyone to leave his money to except Lindsay. But she doesn't want his money."

"Is she nuts?"

"Obviously."

"And then there's this other guy who's into her — I think it's Jake Gyllenhaal. But she's not sure if he only loves her for the millions she's about to inherit. Meanwhile, the stable boy on her grandfather's estate has a huge crush on her."

"So she's got two guys fighting over her," Caitlyn sighed. "I'd settle for just one guy."

So would I, I thought wistfully. *When am I going to meet that one special guy and fall in love? Lindsay's already been "in love" three times this year. I'll settle for once! Isn't it about time?*

As the opening credits for the movie started to appear, I decided I'd forget about my love life and focus on the one on the big screen.

The following morning I was in the kitchen when my father asked, "Where do you think you're going?"

I turned around from the refrigerator, where I was tossing some peaches and plums into my beach bag.

As per Caitlyn's suggestion, I was wearing my yellow one-piece swimsuit. I had a huge straw hat on my head and a huge pair of sunglasses on my face (they were very Mary-Kate and Ashley). I had my blue-and-white striped beach bag tossed over my shoulder and flip-flops on my feet. Um, I was going to the beach. Wasn't it obvious?

My father had that "tone" in his voice. The tone that means even though he's asked you a question, he already knows what he wants your answer to be. He's a lawyer in Manhattan and I know he's used this tone when he's in court. It's why they call him The Shark.

"Caitlyn and I made plans to go to the beach. You know, that place where there's sand and swimming." Suddenly I felt guilty, although I didn't know why. What crime had I committed?

My father shook his head as he sat down at the breakfast table and my mom poured him a cup of coffee. I couldn't help but notice how elegant she looked. She was wearing a very chic gray business suit with her hair in an upsweep. Mom works as an editor at a publishing house in Manhattan and is always lunching or taking meetings with agents and authors.

"No, you're not," he said.

"I'm not? But Caitlyn and I made plans."

"You'll have to make plans for another day."

"But Dad!"

"No buts! At the beginning of the summer you promised that you were going to clean out the garage. Well, the summer is halfway over and we still have a garage filled with junk. I want you to get started on it today."

"Can't I get started on it tomorrow?" I asked.

"Dad says he wants you to do it *today*," Aaron said with a smug smile as he poured some syrup over his pancakes.

I shot a murderous glare at my brother. "I heard what Dad said."

"Then what's the problem?" Michael chimed in. "Rob and I had to paint the house and we're almost finished. Aaron has to mow the front and back lawn every week and he's been doing it. You're the only one who hasn't done what Dad's told you to do. We've been working like dogs and you've been sitting on your butt all summer long."

The murderous glare I had been giving Aaron shifted to Michael. Would it be possible for red lasers to shoot out of my eyes and turn him to dust? It had never happened before, but there's always a first time for everything.

"And I'll bet you've already spent the money he gave you!" Rob added.

"Yeah!" Aaron exclaimed.

"Yeah!" Michael shouted, giving Rob a high five. "I forgot all about that."

At that moment I wanted to reach into my beach bag and throw a piece of fruit at each of my brothers. This is the way it's been my entire life. My three older brothers ganging up on me.

Okay, so they were telling the truth, but still! They made it sound so nasty! They were twisting things around!

At the beginning of the summer, my father had made a deal with the four of us. We'd each been given a paid chore to do and as part of the deal, we were given half of the money in June and would receive the rest once we had finished the task we were assigned. I had been putting off cleaning out the garage because I knew it was going to be dirty, sweaty work and I *hated* dirty, sweaty work.

My father ignored my brothers' comments. "Don't you have plans for tomorrow?"

"I do?"

My father raised his cup of coffee to his mouth and took a sip. "That big clothing sale you've been talking about for weeks. I thought it started tomorrow. Weren't you and Caitlyn going to be the first ones in line?"

I slapped myself on the forehead. "Duh! That's right, it *is* tomorrow."

"How could you forget?" Aaron asked. "There's not much going on up there."

"Aaron, that's enough," my mother warned as she brought a second plate of blueberry pancakes to the table. Within seconds, my brothers' forks had descended into the pile and the plate was empty. Amazing. Simply amazing. You would think they'd never seen food before! And thanks so much for saving some for me! But that's always the way it is with them when it comes to food. They just scarf it down! I wanted to scream, "Taste it! Savor it! Experience the flavors! Food is meant to be *enjoyed*. Don't just inhale it!" Argh! That's why

I don't try my recipes out on them. What's the point if they're not going to try to figure out the ingredients I've used?

"You can choose, Emma," my father said, his voice breaking into my thoughts. "Either you can go to the beach today or you can skip the dress sale tomorrow. But you can't do both, so it's time to decide."

Fifty dollars was waiting for me once the garage was cleaned out. Fifty dollars I could spend tomorrow at H.O.F. This was a no-brainer. "I'll skip the beach," I said, dropping my beach bag to the kitchen floor and heading for the phone in the family room.

"Hey! Princess!" Rob called out, using the nickname I hated. I was so *not* a princess! If I was, I certainly wouldn't be stuck cleaning out the garage on a hot summer day!

"What?" I called back, somewhat crabbily.

"There's no maid service here. Come back and pick up your bag."

I stormed back into the kitchen and picked up my bag, tempted to swing it over my head and bop Rob with it. Instead, I went to the family room and called Caitlyn, telling her I couldn't go to the beach.

"Bummer," she said. "Do you need some help?"

Part of me was touched by her offer to help. At the same time, I was a bit suspicious. Caitlyn and I had been friends for ten years. I knew everything there was to know about her and if there was one thing Caitlyn avoided at all costs, it was hard labor. This was going to require a test.

"That would be great. Thanks. I was hoping Aaron might help but he's not going to be around today. He's going to an amusement park with some friends."

"Can you hold on a second, Em?" Caitlyn put down the phone and I could hear her shouting in the background. "What, Mom? You need me to babysit for cousin Angie? It's kind of short notice, isn't it? Okay, okay, since Angie can't find anyone else, I'll do it." Caitlyn came back on the line. "Sorry, Em. Duty calls."

"Uh-huh," I said knowingly. It's nice to know I can figure Caitlyn out.

"We're still on for the sale tomorrow, right?"

"Of course! You know I wouldn't miss it for the world. We'll talk later and figure out a strategy."

"Okay. Talk to you later."

After getting off the phone with Caitlyn, I went up to my bedroom to change my clothes. I was going to need my grungiest duds. I slipped into a pair of denim shorts with ripped pockets and an oversized T-shirt that had belonged to Rob. The front of the T-shirt said WHAT'S UP, DUDE? Definitely not my finest fashion moment.

When I pushed open the door of the garage, my mouth dropped open. I knew we had been accumulating a lot of junk, but I hadn't realized how much! Where had all this stuff come from?

I didn't know where to begin. There were stacks of magazines and newspapers. Boxes filled with empty bottles. There were old bicycles, sports equipment, cartons of broken toys—I gasped when I peeked into one carton and saw some of my old Barbies with scalped heads! Michael and Aaron had always loved kidnapping my Barbies and cutting off all their hair—trophies, Rollerblades, skateboards, surfboards, old clothes, and baby furniture.

There was even a case of motor oil that had an expiration date of 2000!

How was one person going to be able to handle all this?

Obviously, the sooner I got started, the sooner I would be finished.

Within seconds of lifting my first box, I was sweating. I could feel it dripping down my back and the sides of my face. Ick! The weatherman on the *Today* show had said it was going to go up to ninety degrees today. I could believe it. It already felt like it.

I pulled my hair into two pigtails and tied them back with some string I found. Instantly the back of my neck felt cooler, but I knew that wouldn't last long.

As I kept lugging boxes to the curb, I could see the damage being done to the manicure I had given myself yesterday. The polish on my nails was already chipped. So much for truth in advertising! Then again, I don't think they expected their consumers to be lugging cartons of junk to the curb!

Whenever I was tempted to give up, I kept reminding myself of the prize waiting for me. Fifty dollars to spend tomorrow at H.O.F. Which would be air-conditioned as well! It gave me the strength to go on.

It was after lunch when I decided to carry out the carton of motor oil. Big mistake. Because the cans were leaky. I discovered this when I lifted up the box and felt something oily dribbling down the front of my T-shirt and shorts, leaving two huge streaks.

"Ugh!" I exclaimed, dropping the carton back to the garage floor and wiping my hands across the bottom of my shorts and then mopping at my sweaty forehead. If there's one thing I hate, it's getting dirty. And sweaty. And grubby. I was definitely all three. For the last hour I'd been daydreaming about the bubble bath I was going to give myself once this nightmare project was over. Note to self: Next time Dad asks me to clean out the garage, tell him

I'll do it in the winter.

After dumping the carton of motor oil next to our recycling bin so that my father could take it to the gas station over the weekend, I went back to the garage and found a box of comic books to get rid of. Finding them surprised me. For years Rob had been collecting comics and had gone to all the comics conventions. When had he stopped being into them? I thought about it and realized I hadn't seen him reading a comic book in months. I guess he'd outgrown them since he'd gotten so serious about sports.

I was carrying Rob's comics out of the garage when I started to hear a tearing sound.

Somehow I knew what was going to happen next.

I tried to race to the curb, but I wasn't fast enough and the bottom of the carton broke, spilling comics all across our driveway.

I let out an exasperated sigh before getting down on my knees. I had just started gathering up the spilled comics when I heard a voice ask, "Need some help?"

My hands froze.

I knew that voice.

I instantly recognized it.

No.

No! No! No!

It couldn't be.

Could it?

I lifted my head up slowly, hoping against hope that I was wrong and the voice didn't belong to who I thought it did.

But it did.

It was Kyle.

Once again looking hunky-licious.

While I, on the other hand, looked like Cinderella before the arrival of her fairy godmother!

I was a mess with a capital *M*!

I wanted to disappear.

I wanted a do-over.

This was the second time I was meeting Kyle and I was looking my all-time worst.

"It's Emma, right?"

"Right," I mumbled, keeping my eyes glued to the comics I was collecting. What else was I supposed to do? I looked horrible! The less Kyle saw of me, the better! I just wanted to gather up the comics, throw them out, and then run inside. I'd finish cleaning out the garage later.

But Kyle didn't seem to get the message. Instead, he joined me on the ground and started collecting the spilled comics.

"I've been looking for some of these for ages," he said, his voice filled with excitement. "You weren't going to throw them out, were you?"

I shrugged. "Actually, I was, but you can have them if you want."

"Really?"

There was no mistaking the happiness in Kyle's voice. It made me feel good to make someone else that happy. Who would have thought some old comic books could do that?

"Sure," I answered. "Are you into comics? If you are, you should talk to my brother Rob. He used to go to all the comic book conventions."

Kyle nodded his head. "I'm a comic book junkie. I actually want to be a comic book illustrator one day."

"If comics are your thing, I've got plenty more that I could let you have. Follow me," I said.

As we headed back into the garage, I was having mixed feelings. I mean, in addition to being incredibly hot, Kyle seemed really nice. I was tempted to ask him more about his interests, but then I saw my reflection in an old mirror in a pile of furniture that still needed to be thrown out. I gasped at the image staring back at me, wanting to die of embarrassment!

It was no surprise that I looked as bad as I had expected, but to make matters worse, there was a smudge of grease across my forehead. It must have come from the leaky can of motor oil I had thrown out earlier.

"I need to head inside," I told Kyle, wanting to get as far away from him as possible. It had also just occurred to me that I probably smelled a bit funky from all the hard labor I'd been doing. Not the best way to make a good impression on a guy. "The rest of the comics are in that box." I pointed it out to him. "Just take what you want, okay?"

And with those final words, I left Kyle, vowing that the next time I saw him, he was going to see the AFTER girl and not the BEFORE girl anymore!

Chapter Three

"Mission accomplished," I proudly told my father that night, holding out a palm. "Time to pay up."

During the summer, my dad loves barbecuing. He owns one of those monster grills that all dads in the suburbs have to have. A Weber 3000? Is that what it's called? I'm not exactly sure, but I do know that my dad loves it. And so does my mom because it means she can lounge inside while he cooks. My brothers were in our backyard, sitting around our redwood table, waiting for dinner. Dad was standing at the grill in his "Kiss the Cook" apron, flipping over hamburgers and slathering the spareribs with his supersecret barbecue sauce.

"How about we eat first and then I do an inspection?" he asked. "Deal?"

"Deal!" I agreed, knowing he was going to be pleased by the job I'd done.

Cleaning out the garage had been hard, messy work, but it was over. After my run-in with Kyle, I'd stayed hidden inside for thirty minutes. Then, when I figured the coast was clear, I'd headed back outside and finished emptying out the garage. I'd even swept it clean! I'm very organized, so the rearranging had actually been kind of fun—or, at least, satisfying.

"Wait until you see how much space we have now," I said, pouring myself a glass of lemonade.

"What did you do with my stuff?" Rob asked as he drizzled ranch dressing over his salad.

"Your stuff?" I asked.

"Yeah, my stuff." He passed the bottle of dressing to Michael and started mixing his salad with a fork. "My old skateboard. My Rollerblades. And my comics."

"How about my stuff?" Michael chimed in as he shook the bottle of ranch dressing. "Where'd you put all my old baseball and basketball trophies?"

"And mine?" Aaron asked while picking the tomatoes and red onions out of his salad.

Suddenly I got a bad feeling in the pit of my stomach as three sets of brown eyes stared at me, waiting for my answer.

I gulped, knowing that what I was about to say was so *not* what my brothers were going to want to hear.

"I got rid of it," I whispered.

Rob leaned across the table, cupping a hand to his ear. "I don't think I heard you correctly. What did you say?"

"She said she got rid of it!" Michael yelled.

Rob shoved Michael in the shoulder. "I heard her the first time!"

"Then why did you ask again?" Michael demanded.

"Because I didn't think she'd be stupid

enough to throw out our stuff without asking."

"I'm not stupid!" I shouted, getting angry. Why was I suddenly the bad guy? This *always* happened. My brothers always ganged up on me! "You didn't say that you wanted me to keep anything," I tried to explain. "Otherwise I would have."

"Didn't you stop to think that maybe, just maybe, we might want to keep some of our things?" Rob asked.

"No, I didn't! It's not like I did it on purpose. I thought it was all junk!"

"I bet you didn't throw out any of *your* junk, did you?" Aaron accused, pelting me with a baby tomato that left a stain on my peach shirt.

Actually, I hadn't. I was amazed at some of the stuff I'd found. There had been my first teddy bear. I'd instantly hugged him and put him into an empty box. My Nancy Drew mysteries. I decided to save those, too. And my Little House novels! I had also found the diary I'd kept when I was ten years old. My mouth dropped open when I stumbled upon it. I hadn't seen it in years. How had it wound up in the garage? Making sure no one was around, I had flipped through the pages, skimming over my innermost thoughts and secrets. Some of the things I'd written were *so* embarrassing! This diary was either going to be locked away or I was going to destroy it when I knew no one was around. I certainly didn't want it falling into the wrong hands—my brothers'—so I had put it on top of the box that I had quickly filled, planning to take it up to my bedroom once I had finished.

"She's not answering," Aaron accused. "She saved *her* stuff, but not ours! Princess Emma strikes again."

I hated when my brothers called me Princess or Princess Emma. It made it sound like I was spoiled rotten and I wasn't.

"Dad said to clean out the garage, so I cleaned it out," I said, glowering at Aaron as I dabbed at the tomato stain on my shirt. It had better come out or he was going to pay to have it dry-cleaned. "I'm sorry."

"It's too late for saying sorry," Rob said. "All our things have been carted off to the city dump."

That was true. The garbage men had taken everything away that afternoon. They hadn't looked too happy when they'd seen the piles waiting for them, but that was their job.

"I don't know what else I can do," I said.

"I know what you can do," Rob said. "You can pay me."

"And me!" Michael added.

"And *me*!" Aaron shouted, pelting me with another baby tomato.

I threw the tomato back at Aaron. I was outraged. "*Pay* you?! Are you all crazy? I don't think so. Until today none of you cared about that stuff out in the garage. I'm not paying anything. If you want your things back so badly, you can dig through the city dump."

"You owe us!" Rob shouted.

"I don't owe any of you anything!" I shouted back.

"Oh yes, you do!" Michael shot back.

"Why don't we sell some of her stuff on eBay?" Aaron said, getting up from the table. "Come on! Let's go through her room."

I jumped up out of my seat. "You're not setting one foot in my room!"

"Wanna bet?" Aaron challenged.

Just then my dad returned from the barbecue with a platter of hamburgers and spareribs.

"Aaron, sit down. *Now*," he ordered. "You too, Emma."

Aaron and I both sat back down as my father took his place at the head of the table and started filling his dinner plate.

"Emma is not to blame for your things being thrown out," he said, staring sternly at my three brothers. "You were all sitting at the breakfast table this morning. You have no one to blame but yourselves. If there was anything you wanted saved you should have headed out to the garage and taken it or you should have told Emma not to throw it out. But the three of you didn't do that. And your sister is not a mind reader. So now your things are gone."

"But Dad . . ." Aaron whined.

"No buts!" Dad warned. "This discussion is over. I don't want to hear another word about it."

We ate in silence, my brothers all glaring at me. It wasn't fair! In their minds, they were

55

right and I was wrong. No one ever took my side! It was always me against them. If I'd had three older sisters, I bet none of this would be happening.

After dinner, Dad and I headed out to the garage. He whistled in appreciation as he stared at the empty space. "Nice job, Emma. Very nice. I'm impressed."

"Thanks, Dad."

"So impressed that I'm going to give you an extra twenty-five dollars for the sale tomorrow," he said, reaching into his back pocket for his wallet.

"You don't have to do that," I said.

"I know I don't, but I want to. Hard work deserves to be rewarded. And I think you've earned a bonus having to put up with your brothers."

"I really didn't mean to throw their things out."

"I know you didn't. Don't worry, they'll get over it." My dad checked his watch. "I'm going to head inside. I brought some work home from the office."

I gave my dad a hug. "Thanks for the bonus, Daddy."

He kissed the top of my head as he tucked the money I'd made into my hand. "You earned it, Pumpkin."

After my dad left, I decided to bring the box of things I'd saved that afternoon to my bedroom. I was lifting up the box when I noticed something.

Something that was missing.

I dropped the box to the ground and started pawing through it.

My diary.

Where was it?

I had put it right on top of the box.

And now it was gone!

But not for long.

I knew *exactly* where it was!

I stormed inside the house and went directly to Aaron's room. He was lying on his bed, playing with his Game Boy.

"Give it back!" I demanded in my strongest

tone of voice so he'd know I meant business.

He didn't even look at me, too engrossed in the game of Tetris he was playing. "Give what back?"

"You know what."

He sighed. "I don't have a clue what you're talking about."

"Yes, you do."

I can always tell when Aaron is lying. He avoids looking at you straight in the eye.

Aaron tore his eyes away from his Game Boy, staring directly at me. "I don't know what you're talking about, Emma. Now will you please get lost? I'm still mad at you."

I got the same results with Rob and Michael when I confronted them in the family room, blocking their view of the baseball game that was on TV. They didn't know what I was talking about either.

Now I was really starting to panic.

If my brothers hadn't taken my diary, then where was it?

Where could it have gone?

I was the only one in the garage today.

The only one except . . .

His name popped into my head and I gasped aloud.

Kyle!

Suddenly, I remembered.

The box of stuff I had been saving had been next to Rob's box of comics.

My diary must have fallen into the box of comics that I had given Kyle.

Kyle had my diary!

Five minutes later I was standing on Kyle's front porch, ringing his doorbell. I was definitely not dressed in my most gorgeous, as Caitlyn had suggested. Who had time for clothes or hair and makeup? I was here on a mission. To get my diary back.

I was a nervous wreck, hoping against hope that Kyle hadn't found my diary.

And if he had, that he hadn't read it!

How would I be able to face him if I knew he'd read some of the things I'd written? It would be so embarrassing. More embarrassing than the last two days!

The door opened but instead of facing Kyle I found myself staring down at a little boy who was around five years old. He was adorable! A mini-version of Kyle.

"Who are you?" he asked, sucking on a green lollipop.

"I'm Emma. I live next door."

"What do you want?"

"Is your brother home?"

"KYLE! THERE'S SOMEONE AT THE DOOR FOR YOU!" he yelled at the top of his lungs.

I heard the sound of footsteps coming down a flight of stairs and then Kyle was standing in the doorway. He must have gone to the beach that afternoon because his skin was glowing with a nice golden tan. It made his eyes look even bluer and his blond hair blonder.

Stop! I scolded myself. *Must stop drooling over Kyle! Must focus on retrieving lost diary! Once diary is retrieved, then I can return to going ga-ga over Kyle!*

"Hey, Emma." He gave me a smile and I wondered if it was possible to be blinded by shiny white teeth. "I see you got to meet my little brother, Tommy."

My ears were still ringing from Tommy's powerful lungs.

"Yes, I have." I gave Tommy a smile but he didn't smile back. He sucked on his lollipop, staring at me suspiciously.

"So what's up?" Kyle asked.

I didn't know where to begin.

I couldn't tell him the truth.

So I decided to lie.

I never like lying. But this wasn't a *real* lie.

"Remember those comic books I gave you this afternoon?"

"Kyle collects comic books," Tommy said, crunching on his lollipop. "I can't read yet but I can look at the pictures. Sometimes Kyle reads his comic books to me. Right, Kyle?"

Kyle ran a hand through Tommy's hair. "Right, Squirt."

"Uh, about the comics," I said, starting to feel uncomfortable. I wanted to get this conversation over with!

Kyle's face lit up. "Thanks again. I haven't had a chance to go through them yet. After I got home, I took Tommy and my little sister, Megan, to Jones Beach."

He hadn't gone through the box yet! Yes!

"I have to take them back," I said in a rush. "They belonged to my brother Rob and I gave them away without checking to see if it was okay. He wants them back."

Kyle's face froze. "Take them back?"

"No!" Tommy shouted, throwing his half-eaten lollipop at me. It stuck to the front of my shirt. Great. Now I had a lollipop stain to go with my tomato stain. "You can't have them back. You can't! They're Kyle's! KYLE'S!!!" Tommy threw himself down on the floor and began kicking with his feet. In a matter of seconds, his face turned beet red as he started screaming, "MOMMY! THERE'S A MEAN GIRL WHO'S TAKING AWAY KYLE'S COMICS!!!"

"But I have to get them back," I said, trying not to sound desperate and wondering why I was explaining myself to a five-year-old who was having a temper tantrum.

Tommy jumped back on his feet. "I don't

like you! You're mean. MEEEEAN!!!"

With those final words Tommy ran back into the house, still screaming that I was mean.

Even though I had just met Tommy, his words cut into my heart. Little kids always loved me and now here was one who hated me.

"So Rob wants his comics back?" Kyle asked, the smile on his face gone.

"Uh-huh."

"Then how come he didn't ask for them himself?"

"What?"

"When I was taking out the garbage after dinner, I saw Rob in your driveway and I thanked him for the comics. He told me to enjoy them. If he wanted them back, why didn't he just ask for them himself?"

This is why I never lie. Because there's always the chance of getting caught!

I didn't know what to say that would make sense. I guess I could tell Kyle the truth but I felt it was a little too late for the truth. I shrugged. "I don't know. Maybe he was embarrassed. Actually, he didn't tell me to ask for them back. He was mad that I gave them away so I thought I would surprise him by giving them back."

"So why didn't you just say that?"

Kyle didn't give me a chance to answer. He turned his back on me and headed into the house. When he returned, he handed me the box of comic books. Was it my imagination or had he shoved them at me? He certainly hadn't handed them over gently.

"If you'd just let me explain," I began. "This time I promise to tell you the truth."

"Save it, Emma. You wanted the comics back and now you have them."

And with those final words, Kyle closed the front door, leaving me all alone on his front porch.

As I walked down the front steps, back to my house, I heard the sound of tapping behind me. Thinking it was Kyle, I turned around eagerly.

But it wasn't Kyle.

Instead it was Tommy, his face pressed

against the living room window, sticking his tongue out at me.

I felt horrible.

I was going to have to make things up to Kyle in some way, but how?

I'd definitely have to pick Caitlyn's brain tomorrow when we were shopping.

As I had suspected, my diary had fallen into the box of comics. It was wedged all the way at the bottom on its side. After retrieving it, I began tearing the pages into teeny tiny pieces. Aaron's been known to go through my trash and I never underestimate him.

When I had finished destroying my diary, I decided to go online and check my high school email account. All incoming freshmen at North Marshall High were assigned one and when I inherited the Dear Daisy column I was told that whenever a question was sent to Daisy, I would be sent an automatic email. Even though classes didn't start for another month, I wanted to make sure it was working. So I sent an email from my home account to my high school account.

When I accessed my email, I was stunned to find not only the email I had just sent, but an automatic email as well.

Which meant that someone had already posted a question to Dear Daisy!

My mouth dropped open. Who could be writing to Daisy in the summer?

All sorts of horrible scenarios raced through my mind until I calmed myself down and went to the Dear Daisy blog.

When I opened up the email from Romeo14, I was stunned to see it was from a guy!

> Hey! So I was just checking out the NMH site for the first time and I came across your blog. Are you like the Dear Abby of our school? My grandmother loves reading her. I think Dear Abby is dead though and someone else writes the column. Is that the deal with you or are you for real? Anyway, I'm not sure if anyone's even checking this blog, since it's the summer, but I figured I'd give it a shot. So, uh, if anyone's out there, I need advice! I met

this beautiful girl but she gave me the cold
shoulder. Is it worth pursuing her? Romeo

I exhaled. Phew! This I could handle. I
didn't even have to think about an answer. My
fingers quickly flew over my keyboard.

Dear Romeo: Girls who are icy don't play
nicey-nicey. I suggest you say adios to this
ice princess and find yourself a girl with a
warm, loving heart! xoxox, Daisy

After sending Daisy's reply, I turned off my
computer and turned on the TV, flipping to
Soap Net, my favorite channel. *All My Children*
was just starting and I wanted to see what
Erica was up to today. But even though *AMC* is
my favorite soap, I had a hard time watching.
Thoughts of Kyle kept slipping into my mind
and stayed there until I turned off the lights
and tried to go to sleep.

Chapter Four

The following morning Caitlyn and I were among the very first in line for the House of Fashion summer sale. We'd gotten a ride from Rob before he'd gone to his job as a golf caddy at the country club. Naturally he had to grumble and complain when I asked if he could drop us off. Like it was such a big deal! The mall is right on his way to the country club.

Usually Caitlyn and I will take the bus to the mall, but we wanted to get there super early. Definitely before House of Fashion opened its doors. Believe me, if I could have avoided traveling in Rob's car, I would have. That's because his car, like his bedroom, is a pigsty. Scattered on the floor of his car are wrappers and soda containers from fast-food restaurants. There's the usual sports equipment, as well as unwashed T-shirts, socks, and shorts. The air in his car stinks—sorry, there's no other way to say it!—and when we're driving I keep my window rolled down, even when it's hot in the summer. He won't let me touch his radio and instead of listening to my favorites like Kelly Clarkson or Beyoncé, we have to listen to the sports station.

After Rob dropped us off at the mall, Caitlyn and I walked inside. We were expecting the mall to be pretty deserted since it was so early, but as we got closer and closer to H.O.F., we could see that a line had already formed outside its grated front.

"I can't believe other people got here before us!" Caitlyn exclaimed as she counted the number of shoppers ahead of us. "There are at least ten people and it's not even nine o'clock."

"Maybe some of them work for the store," I suggested.

"Then why haven't they let them inside?"

I shrugged. "Let's look at the bright side. At least we're not at the end of the line."

Since Caitlyn and I had arrived, another twenty-five girls had gotten in line behind us. And the line kept getting longer and longer.

"Looks like we're going to have some serious competition," Caitlyn said worriedly, chewing on her lower lip.

"But we have the advantage," I reminded her. "They don't have a shopping strategy the way we do."

Caitlyn and I had been coming to H.O.F. for the last week, scoping out the store. Like I mentioned earlier, I'm hyper-organized. We've been to these sales before and you need to have a game plan. If you don't, you're toast. We had a plan. I'd make sure of it. Caitlyn had grumbled—she hates shopping without buying and we'd been to H.O.F. three times in the last week—but I knew she'd thank me once she had a shopping bag of reduced-price merchandise.

We knew the entire layout of the store and we already had our eye on a couple of things. Dresses were in the back of the store while skirts and jeans were at the front of the store. Sweaters, blouses, tops, and vests were in the middle of the store. The shoe department was on the second floor, as well as accessories like purses, belts, scarves, and jewelry. Fall wear was also on the second floor, as well as the last of the summer merchandise.

There were two skirts that I was going to make a beeline for as soon as the doors opened. A girl can never have enough jeans so I would be stocking up on those. Then I would move on to a couple of tops that I thought were cute before finally tackling the shoe department.

When I shop, I shop with a mission. I keep in mind what I already own and try to add to my wardrobe by mixing and matching so I can come up with as many outfits as possible. This is because I have to be selective. As much as I would love to buy everything that I try on, I can't afford it. Unlike some of the girls I go to school with, who already have their own credit cards (!) or get to use their parents' cards, it doesn't work that way at my house. My brothers and I have always had to earn the things we want. We get a weekly allowance, but we also have part-time jobs. I babysit, while Michael works at a video store and Aaron delivers pizzas. When Rob's away at college he works at the campus bookstore.

That's not to say that when it's our birthday or Christmas, Mom and Dad don't splurge on us. They do. It's just that they want us to learn how to save and spend our money wisely.

My brothers like to call me a shopaholic.

To a certain degree, it's true.

I love shopping.

Oooh, shopping! I'm getting tingles just thinking about it.

The fun of discovery!

The joy of trying on new clothes and seeing how they look!

The thrill of victory, walking out of a store with a shopping bag full of clothes that are *yours*!

My favorite novels are the Sophie Kinsella *Shopaholic* novels, starring Becky Bloomwood.

Yes, I identify with Becky and her love of shopping. But unlike Becky, I have total control over my spending.

"What are you going to do about Kyle?" Caitlyn asked, breaking into my thoughts.

I had filled Caitlyn in on the latest with Kyle on our drive to the mall.

"I don't know."

"Do you like him?"

"How can I like him? I hardly even know him! He just moved in next door."

"But you think he's cute, right?"

"Yes," I admitted, remembering Kyle's blue eyes and his dazzling smile. "I think he's cute."

"Maybe when we finish up here, we can head back to your house. Maybe we'll run into him. I'm dying to meet him."

For some reason, I felt a pang of jealousy at those words. Which was crazy. What did I have to be jealous about? Nothing. Besides, Caitlyn had a crush on Aaron, although I couldn't understand why.

But I wondered, *Would Kyle like Caitlyn better than me? Would he think she was prettier?*

"Isn't that the top you were looking at the other day?" Caitlyn asked, pointing to a yellow wrap chiffon blouse in the window.

"Shhh!" I scolded Caitlyn, slapping down her hand while looking around to make sure no one else had seen what she'd done. "Lower your voice." One of the first rules of shopping during a sale is to not let the other shoppers know what you're interested in. If someone else knows you want it, they're going to go after it! Sounds crazy, but it's true.

"It looks like they're getting ready to open the doors!" Caitlyn squealed excitedly as the line in front of us began moving and the heavy metal grate in front of the store slowly rose upward.

Once the doors opened, the line rushed straight into the store. Within seconds it was a madhouse! Girls were everywhere: running, shrieking, and grabbing, grabbing, grabbing!

Hangers were flying off the racks.

Stacks of sweaters and jeans tumbled to the floor.

Lines were already forming outside the dressing rooms.

Each and every girl was on a mission.

Including me!

I began gathering up the clothes I was interested in. Everything was where I remembered.

Except for the top in the window.

It was gone.

I couldn't help but feel disappointed. It was just like the top I'd seen Mischa Barton wearing in the latest issue of *In Touch*. Why hadn't I snatched it up first?

But just because the top was gone, that didn't mean I still didn't have a chance at it. I'd been to too many of these sales not to know how they worked. Sometimes when someone picked up an item, they later decided they didn't want it, or after trying it on they didn't like the way it looked and they just tossed it onto a rack.

If I kept my eyes open, there was a good chance I'd spot my blouse.

For now, I had plenty to try on. I headed off to the nearest dressing room with my haul, joined by Caitlyn who had a stack of her own.

We spent the next two hours trying on outfits.

Luckily, Caitlyn and I are both the same size, so we were able to pass clothes back and forth to each other. If there was something I'd picked out and I didn't like the way it looked on me, Caitlyn tried it on. And vice versa. Plus, since we're always borrowing each other's clothes, we got to double our wardrobes. It was like we were doing twice the shopping for half the cost!

Finally, we each decided on what we were going to buy. In my pile I had a plum velvet jacket, an ultraglam white cloth coat, a pair of jeans painted with tiny butterflies, a sky blue blouse, a short, pleated skirt in a purple-and-black plaid, a chocolate brown fake suede skirt, and a fake cashmere turtleneck sweater in black.

Caitlyn had found a pink linen dress that came with a matching jacket that tied with a pink ribbon, a pair of flared jeans, a turquoise blazer, a fake camel-hair skirt, a black pleated skirt, and a silk-and-lace camisole top. (I knew my dad would *never* let me wear a top like that. Maybe when I was sixteen. But not at fourteen! I had a feeling Caitlyn would be returning the top to the store. Or at least giving it to her older sister, Tess, who would be a senior, once her father saw it. I told her not to buy it, but she wouldn't listen.)

As for the shoes . . .

The one thing House of Fashion is known for are their cheap shoes. Yes, cheap. But sturdy! Their shoes always last. They're designer knockoffs that look like the real thing, and from poring over the pages of *Vogue*, I know the real thing.

Until the day comes that I can afford a real pair of Jimmy Choos or Manolo Blahniks (yes, I also watch *Sex and the City*, but the edited version that's badly dubbed and makes me wonder what Carrie and her girlfriends originally said), H.O.F. will have to do.

Caitlyn and I were both in heaven! I found a pair of red-and-white polka dot kitten heels, yellow gingham ankle straps (which would have been *so* perfect with the yellow top from the window!), and light-green crystal-studded slides. Caitlyn found a pair of wedges decorated with ladybugs, striped cotton slides, and flats with a garden print. Neither one of us felt like buying any "practical" shoes.

"I don't think I can carry anything else," Caitlyn said as we headed in the direction of the cash registers at the back of the store.

"I can!" I exclaimed as I spotted my blouse from the window hanging on a rack with other abandoned clothing.

I quickly snatched it up and checked the size. It was a small. Yes! Now I could go home *extremely* happy. I'd gotten everything I wanted.

I was waiting in line to pay for my clothes when suddenly I felt a poke in the shoulder. Since the store was packed with so many shoppers, I ignored it, figuring someone had bumped into me.

But then there it was again.

A poke.

Only harder than the last one I'd received.

I turned around, facing a skinny girl with frizzy blond hair, freckles, and round granny glasses. She looked familiar but I couldn't remember where I had seen her before.

"I had that first," she said, pointing to the yellow top I had just found. "You *stole* it from me."

The other girls in line stopped talking, turning to look at me and the other girl, waiting to see what was going to happen next.

"I didn't steal it from you," I said. "I found it abandoned on a rack."

"That's right," Caitlyn said, backing me up. "She found it."

"It wasn't abandoned. I put it there. I was on the other side of the rack. Now are you going to give me back my top or am I going to have to *take* it back?"

Staring into her mean face, I suddenly remembered where I'd last seen Miss Frizz.

She'd been standing behind me and Caitlyn when we were waiting for the store to open.

She'd been eavesdropping on our conversation.

She'd seen Caitlyn point out the blouse.

I wasn't the blouse stealer.

She was!

"This girl is a blouse stealer!" Miss Frizz started yelling. "She stole my blouse! It's not like she doesn't have enough things to buy. Oh no! Look at her! Loaded down with practically half the store! All I wanted to do was buy one measly top and I can't even have that!"

I've never stolen anything in my entire life and to be accused of stealing in front of complete strangers? It was mortifying!

I knew I was right and Miss Frizz was wrong, but I just wanted an end to this whole ugly mess. I hate being the center of attention and right now practically everyone in House of Fashion was staring at me. I was just about to hand over the top so Miss Frizz would shut up when I heard a voice behind me.

It was loud.

Extremely loud.

And familiar.

Very familiar.

"KYLE! IT'S THAT MEAN GIRL! EMMA! SHE TOOK AWAY THAT GIRL'S SHIRT JUST LIKE SHE TOOK AWAY YOUR COMIC BOOKS LAST NIGHT!"

I wanted to die.

At that very second all I wanted to do was disappear.

All conversations stopped.

Everyone looked in my direction.

Including Kyle, who was staring at me, his mouth hanging open in shock as he looked from me, with my monstrous pile of clothing and my three boxes of shoes, to Miss Frizz, who was standing empty-handed in front of me.

How much of the conversation had he over-heard?

I wanted to explain myself.

I wanted to tell him that what he was hear-ing wasn't true.

I hadn't stolen anything!

I was innocent.

Falsely accused of a crime I didn't commit!

But before I could say anything, Kyle was joined by an older woman carrying an H.O.F. shopping bag and a little girl around the age of seven. It had to be Kyle's mother and sister. They all looked so much alike.

Before I could say anything, Kyle followed after his mother and sister. As they headed out of the store, I could hear Tommy shout, "WHY'S EMMA STEALING THAT GIRL'S CLOTHES, KYLE? WHY'S SHE SO MEAN? MEAN, MEAN, MEAN!"

At that moment I desperately wished for a lollipop to stick in Tommy's mouth.

Chapter Five

I never wanted to see a yellow chiffon wrap blouse again.

Unfortunately, I was the proud owner of one.

As was Miss Frizz.

While the blouse battle was unfolding, bringing all activity at House of Fashion to a halt, a store manager with silver hair teased into a big poofy cloud, wearing what looked like a *real* Chanel suit (obviously *not* purchased at H.O.F.), had ducked into a back storeroom and found another five yellow chiffon wrap blouses, three smalls and two larges. She'd proudly given one to Miss Frizz and one to me, telling us that we could both buy one.

After all the drama that had gone on, what was I supposed to do? Tell her I didn't want it?

I couldn't.

She seemed so pleased that she had solved the problem.

So I bought it.

And I never planned to wear it again.

How could I? Every time Kyle saw me wearing it, he'd think I'd stolen it from Miss Frizz! And if he didn't, I'm sure Tommy's big mouth would remind him that I had.

I shoved the top to the back of my closet and took a deep cleansing breath, deciding to focus on my other purchases. One of the best parts of a shopping spree is coming home with your new things and rearranging your closet. The new clothes go in front, the clothes you wear a lot get shifted to the middle, and the clothes you rarely wear get shoved to the back, never to see the light of day again.

The first thing I decided to try on was the

faux cashmere black turtleneck. I paired it with a white miniskirt that I already owned, added a thin chain metal belt around my waist, wide silver hoops to my ears, and slipped into a pair of knee-high white boots. Inspecting myself in the full-length mirror on the back of my bedroom door, I was very pleased with the results. The look was very mod. Very 60s. A few seasons ago on *America's Next Top Model*, the girls had gone to London and in one of the challenges they'd had to outfit themselves in mod fashion. None of them had had a clue! If I'd been on the show, I would have nailed the challenge!

I was just about to change into another outfit when I noticed a burning smell in the air.

Opening my bedroom door, I went out into the hallway, where the smell was even stronger. Had one of my brothers left a bag of microwave popcorn in the microwave for too long?

I headed downstairs to the kitchen, sniffing the air. But when I got into the kitchen, no one was there and nothing was burning.

So where was the smell coming from?

All the windows in the house were open, so it had to be coming from outside.

I stepped out onto the back porch and that's when I saw it.

Smoke coming out of Kyle's kitchen window!

I instantly ran inside and grabbed our fire extinguisher, then ran next door.

By the time I got there, Kyle was standing on his back porch, a funnel of black smoke billowing out of his kitchen, holding a roasting pan with a burnt roast in his oven-mitted hands. Standing behind him, waving at the air and coughing, were Tommy and Megan.

"What are you doing?" I asked. "Trying to burn your house down?"

"I'm trying to make a roast," Kyle said.

"Do you like your meat well done?"

"I don't know what I did wrong. The recipe said to sear the meat at five hundred degrees."

"For fifteen minutes," I finished. "Then you turn the temperature down to about three fifty and cook the roast for twenty minutes per pound."

"You're supposed to do that?"

"Didn't you read the entire recipe?"

"Er, no. I kind of skimmed it."

"And that's why you're holding a burnt roast in your hands," I explained, peeking into the roasting pan and pointing at what looked like rocks. "What are those black things?"

"They were supposed to be baked potatoes."

"If you don't mind my asking, why are you trying to make like a chef?"

"It's my parents' wedding anniversary tonight. I wanted to surprise them with dinner."

My heart instantly melted. That was *so* sweet! My parents were lucky if my brothers even remembered to give them a card!

"What's *she* doing here?" Tommy whined.

I couldn't believe it. This kid must hate me!

"What did you come to take *this* time?" he demanded.

Ouch! That Tommy sure knew how to deliver a zinger!

"I smelled smoke and came to make sure everything was okay," I explained to Tommy, giving him a smile.

He didn't smile back.

"You better not take any of my toys," he warned.

"I'm not going to take your toys."

"How come you're dressed so funny?" he asked.

Why was it every time I got into a conversation with Tommy, I had to explain myself?

"I think she looks pretty," Megan said shyly.

"You look silly," Tommy said.

Silly? I looked *silly*?! I looked fabulous! Models in magazines wore outfits like the one I was wearing! What did a five-year-old know about fashion?!

"I like your earrings," Megan said, her first words directed to me so far. "They're pretty."

"Would you like to try them on?" I asked, taking them off.

"Can I?" she asked, her face lighting up with joy.

"Sure," I said, slipping them into her pierced ears.

At least one of Kyle's siblings liked me.

Now I'd just have to work on Tommy.

"I guess it's back to the drawing board," Kyle sighed, heading into the kitchen.

"Why don't I give you a little help this time?" I suggested, following after him while Tommy stuck to Kyle like glue, still eyeing me warily, as Megan followed in my footsteps.

Old Mrs. Winslow had lived in Kyle's house until she'd moved to Florida to live with her daughter and grandchildren two years ago. My brothers and I used to visit all the time and she would always have a cookie jar filled with oatmeal cookies for us. Sometimes we'd even bake together. Some of my earliest memories are when Mrs. Winslow used to babysit for me and my brothers. She'd take me into the kitchen and I'd sit on a stool and watch her make a cake or a pie from scratch. I was always amazed at how she could take a bunch of different ingredients and make something delicious. My interest in cooking started with her.

When I stepped inside, I was totally amazed by the kitchen I was seeing. When Mrs. Winslow had lived in the house, the kitchen had looked like something out of the 1950s, with a linoleum floor, wallpaper decorated with fruit, cabinets with squares of glass, a white rusty sink, an old-fashioned stove and refrigerator, and an aluminum table and chairs.

Kyle's parents had totally renovated the kitchen. Now there were stainless-steel appliances, including a huge stove, refrigerator, dishwasher, and microwave. The sink was also stainless steel, but one of those double ones, and the cabinets were cherry wood with shiny brass handles. The floors were gleaming hardwood and the walls were painted a creamy white with yellow trim. There were rag rugs on the floor and, in the center of the room, there was a huge oval table and chairs made of oak with a brightly colored Tiffany lamp hanging over it.

The kitchen looked exactly like the ones in those decorating magazines my mom always reads.

Except for one little thing.

It also looked like a disaster area.

Every surface of the kitchen was covered with used pots, pans, and cooking utensils. Both sides of the sink were filled with dirty dishes and glasses. An open bag of flour was scattered across the counter. There were piles of chopped vegetables, open bottles of oil, vinegar, and other spices, as well as an overflowing garbage can.

"What happened in here?" I gasped.

Kyle ran a hand across the back of his neck. "Things kind of got out of control," he said sheepishly.

"I was helping," Megan explained, tossing her head back and forth so she could swing my earrings.

"Kyle's lucky you were helping him," I said.

Tommy stuck his head out from behind Kyle's legs. "I was helping too!" he huffed, scrunching up his face in outrage that Megan hadn't mentioned his name.

"What else were you making?" I asked Kyle.

"Stuffed mushrooms, broccoli with lemon juice, and crescent rolls."

I stared at the pile of flour. "You were making crescent rolls from scratch?"

"Yeah. Why?"

"Ever hear of the Pillsbury Doughboy? Does commercials on TV? You can buy crescent rolls at the supermarket. No fuss. In ten minutes you have perfect rolls." I stared at a pile of chopped chocolate. "What were you making for dessert?"

"Chocolate soufflé."

My mouth dropped open. "Think you could have started with something a little harder?"

"I thought I could handle it."

I waved an arm around the messy kitchen. "I think you might have been wrong."

"Obviously," Kyle sighed. "What am I going to do? My mom's at the beauty parlor for another two hours. I wanted everything to be ready by the time she got back."

"Can I ask you a question?"

"Shoot."

"Have you ever cooked before?"

"Nope."

"Then what made you think you could cook an anniversary dinner for your parents? And one that was so complicated!"

"They make it look so easy on the Food Channel."

I laughed. "They're supposed to—that way people will buy their videos and books. Beware of perky chefs on the Food Channel! Since this was your first time cooking, you should probably have stuck with the basics. That's the first thing they teach you in cooking class. Then you can work your way up to more complicated dishes."

"You've taken cooking classes?"

"Uh-huh. Last fall."

"That's how you knew about searing the meat."

"Yep."

"So, what should I make instead?"

I rolled up the sleeves of my turtleneck. "Why don't we clean up first and then we'll come up with a menu. If we all work together, I'm sure we can get everything under control."

"Thanks for helping me out, Emma."

"Hey," I said, grinning to myself while filling the sink with hot water and adding a squirt of dishwashing liquid that instantly turned to suds, "that's what neighbors are for."

It took an hour, but the kitchen no longer looked like a disaster area. Everything was cleaned up and put away. I, on the other hand, looked a mess. No surprise there. It seemed to be a requirement whenever I was around Kyle. My new turtleneck was covered with flour, as well as all other sorts of culinary gook. Oh well, it would wash out. And if it didn't, it had only cost me ten bucks! At least, by some miracle, my white skirt didn't have a stain on it.

"I'm going to go home and change into a pair of shorts and a T-shirt," I said. "Then we'll head down to the supermarket. It's on Second Street. Have you been yet?"

"I haven't had a chance to do much exploring since we moved in."

"I'll give you a mini-tour on the way."

"I don't want to go to the store," Tommy announced as he walked over to the refrigerator, pulled up a chair, and took a cherry Popsicle out of the freezer. "I want to stay home and watch TV."

"Sorry, Squirt," Kyle said. "You're too little

to stay home by yourself."

I was going to get Tommy to like me no matter how hard I had to try. "They have a motorcycle ride at the supermarket. If you're good, I'll buy you a ride."

"Two rides," Tommy shot back, sucking on his Popsicle.

"Okay, two rides." If it took two rides to get him to like me, then I would buy him two rides.

"We'll meet you out front in ten minutes," Kyle said.

I raced out the kitchen door. "See you in a bit!"

I love grocery shopping.

Aisle after aisle of bright, colorful boxes and shiny cellophane-wrapped packages.

Filled with all sorts of yummy treats.

Whenever I have a cart in a supermarket, I just want to fill it up.

I couldn't do that today, though.

I was here to help Kyle with his dinner, so we had to just get the basics.

Tommy, however, disagreed. Every chance

he got, he would throw something into our cart. And Kyle would promptly take it out.

"I want this cereal!" Tommy said, racing up to our cart when we were in the cookie aisle and holding up a box of Count Chocula.

"Mom doesn't want you eating cereal like that. Only Corn Flakes or Rice Krispies. You know that."

"How about these for a snack?" I asked, trying to keep the peace and holding up a packet of Mini Oreos. "My treat."

Tommy made a face, like I had suggested he eat garbage. "Yuck! I don't like Oreos."

"Ritz crackers filled with peanut butter?" I suggested, scanning the shelves. There were so many choices. There had to be something here that he liked!

"Peanut butter makes me throw up."

"It does not!" Megan said.

"Does too!"

"Megan, would you like some cookies?" I asked.

"No, thank you."

Such an angel!

"Pecan Sandies?" I asked the mini-demon.

"I don't want cookies! I WANT CEREAL!!!"

Ah! We were back to the shouting. How I had missed it!

"Knock it off!" Kyle warned sternly. "We are not buying cereal, Squirt! Emma offered to buy you some cookies and you turned her down. I don't want to hear another word out of you. We're here to buy groceries for Mom and Dad's dinner and that's it."

Obviously Tommy knew not to mess with Kyle because he didn't say another word as we went from aisle to aisle.

"I think we have everything we need," I told Kyle. "We just have to get some fruit for the fruit salad and we'll be all set."

After filling our cart with a carton of strawberries, blueberries, raspberries, and a bunch of green grapes, all that was left was the cantaloupe. I started squeezing them, looking for one that was firm, but not too firm, and reached for one at the exact same time as a little old lady who was also squeezing them.

"Better let her have the cantaloupe," Kyle warned her, pointing at me and shaking his head knowingly. "You don't want to mess with her. I've seen her do battle over a shirt."

"YEAH!" Tommy shouted, choosing that moment to break his silence.

I instantly dropped the cantaloupe I was holding.

At that moment, I wanted to race out of the supermarket.

Until I saw the teasing smile on Kyle's face.

He was just messing around with me.

What a relief! At least, I thought.

"If I were you, I wouldn't be so quick to judge," I sassed back, giving the little old lady a smile and handing her the cantaloupe I'd dropped back into the pile. "I've seen how guys get when the new Xboxes go on sale. Worse than girls!"

After finding a cantaloupe, we paid for our groceries and headed back to Kyle's house. Tommy and Megan were given a video to watch in the living room while I gave Kyle a lesson in Cooking 101.

The menu was simple: roast chicken (just clean it and stick it in the oven), mashed potatoes (peel them, cut them, boil them for a long while, and then mash them with butter and milk), string beans (snap them, boil them for only two minutes, then add a dash of salt and pepper), crescent rolls (courtesy of Pillsbury!), and a fruit salad for dessert (just slice up the cantaloupe and throw it into a bowl with all the other fruit).

While I was showing Kyle how it was all done, I filled him in on the teachers at North Marshall High, telling him which ones were the favorites and which ones weren't. I also told him about all the after-school clubs, as well as where the local sport center and movie theaters were.

"You're not happy about having moved, are you?" I asked. I don't know what made me ask that question, but suddenly Kyle had gotten quiet.

He shrugged. "I wouldn't say I'm unhappy. I just miss my friends, you know? Talking about school made me think about them. I thought we were going to be freshmen together and we're not."

"You'll make new friends."

"I know."

"Maybe we'll be in some classes together," I said.

"Yeah, maybe."

"You're going to like living here, Kyle," I insisted, wanting to cheer him up, but not knowing what else to say. Suddenly there was an awkward silence and I *hate* awkward silences.

I wiped my hands on a dish towel. "Well, it looks like you're all set for dinner. All you have to do is take the chicken out at six o'clock. Then you can just heat up the mashed potatoes and string beans. The rolls are easy. Just pop them on a cookie sheet and stick them in the oven."

"Thanks for all your help, Emma. I really appreciate it. You make it all look so easy."

I tried not to blush but I could feel my cheeks turning red. "Anytime! If you want some more cooking lessons, let me know. And if there's anything else I can do, you just have to ask me."

"Actually, there is."

"Really?"

He's going to say he wants to thank me for helping him out and ask me if I want to go to a movie. Yes, that's it! We're just going to go as friends, of course, but that doesn't mean we can't eventually become more than friends!

"It's kind of a favor."

I snapped back to reality. Favors didn't involve sitting in the dark in a movie theater with a cute guy and a tub of buttered popcorn.

"What kind of favor?"

"Would you mind babysitting Megan and Tommy tonight? I want to give my folks a romantic evening alone. I figure I would serve them dinner and then clean up and they could have some time to themselves. They can't if Tommy and Megan are around. Megan's usually no hassle, but you've seen Tommy. He's a handful."

That was putting it mildly!

How could I say no? I couldn't. And I *was* a babysitter. Although I wouldn't think of charging Kyle!

"I'd be happy to watch them. Free of charge. I'll swing by at six?"

"Great!"

I had a feeling Tommy wasn't going to think it was so great when he found out who he was going to be spending his evening with. . . .

Chapter Six

"Bowling is fun, Tommy. You'd like it if you tried it."

"No! I don't want to bowl." Tommy folded his arms over his chest and glared at me stubbornly. "AND YOU CAN'T MAKE ME!!!"

"Stop being such a baby," Megan said as she threw her bowling ball down the alley.

"I'M NOT A BABY! I'M A BIG BOY!"

Is this what I had to look forward to when I was a mother twenty years from now? If so, staying single was starting to look pretty good!

I had decided, rather than just bringing Megan and Tommy over to my house to watch a video, I would do something fun with them and take them bowling.

When I rang the bell at Kyle's house at six o'clock, Tommy was the one who opened the front door. As soon as he saw me, his eyes widened like huge saucers.

"What do *you* want?"

I loved how he could put so much contempt into one little word.

I knelt down to Tommy's level and gave him a big smile. "I'm going to babysit you and Megan tonight."

Within seconds, a look of horror washed over Tommy's face.

"OH NO, YOU'RE NOT!"

And he slammed the door in my face.

I rang the bell again.

"GO AWAY!" he shouted. "WE DON'T WANT ANY!"

I heard Kyle behind the door. "What's going on, Squirt? Who's at the door?"

"Kyle, it's me," I called out. "Emma. Reporting for babysitting duty."

Kyle opened the front door and gave me a smile. "I think I can figure out what just happened."

"Tell her to go away!"

"No can do, Squirt. Emma is going to watch you and Megan tonight while Mom and Dad have their anniversary dinner. I have to stay here and serve it."

Tommy opened his mouth and took a deep breath, preparing to let it all out in what I was sure would be a loud scream. But Kyle foiled him, putting a hand over his mouth.

"Excuse us, Emma. Tommy and I need to have a man-to-man talk."

Kyle took Tommy off to one side and started whispering to him. Tommy kept shaking his head. He stamped his foot once or twice until finally, after Kyle gave him a disappointed look, I heard him say, "Okay, Kyle."

I don't know what Kyle said to him, but a new-and-improved Tommy was returned to me.

"Megan!" Kyle called out. "Emma is here."

Megan came running down the front stairs with a smile on her face. At least she was glad to see me!

"I thought we'd go bowling tonight," I told Megan and Tommy. "Wouldn't that be fun?"

"I like bowling," Megan said.

Tommy remained silent.

"Well, why don't we head out?" I held a hand out to both Megan and Tommy. Megan took my hand but Tommy didn't take mine. Instead, after looking at my hand like it was unwashed, he slipped his hand into Megan's. Oooh, he really knew how to zing me!

"Be good," Kyle called out. "Remember, Santa's always watching."

Aha! Santa! I'd have to remember that for future use!

"If I finish up here early, maybe I'll stop by the alley," Kyle told me. "Otherwise I'll see you when you bring them back."

"Okay," I said, hoping that Kyle would be able to make it.

As we walked to the bowling alley, Megan

talked nonstop, telling me all about her dolls and toys and favorite books. I tried to talk to Tommy, asking him what his favorite toys and books were, but he ignored me. Well, at least silence was better than screaming.

Unfortunately, the silence didn't last very long.

The problems started again at the alley after we'd gotten to our lane and bumpers were put in so the balls wouldn't go into the gutters. I figured Megan and Tommy would have more fun this way and they'd get to hit pins.

I helped Megan put on her bowling shoes and then turned to Tommy, who tucked his legs under himself.

"I'm not putting on those shoes," he said, making a face. "They smell."

I stuck my nose into a shoe. Okay, so he had a point. But he couldn't bowl unless he wore the shoes, I explained to him. He didn't want to hear it.

"You know, Tommy," I said, shaking my head sadly, "I don't think Santa would be happy if he knew you were breaking the rules at the bowling alley."

Instantly, Tommy's legs came out from under him, his sneakers came off, and the bowling shoes went on.

That didn't mean he was going to bowl, of course.

Resulting in the latest scream-fest.

I didn't want the little guy to be miserable all night. What could I do to make him happy? Out of the corner of my eye, I saw the bright lights of the bowling alley's concession stand.

"Would you like an ice-cream cone?" I asked.

Tommy slowly nodded his head.

At last. Success!

"What kind do you want?"

"A vanilla-and-chocolate-swirl cone with sprinkles."

"One vanilla-and-chocolate-swirl cone with sprinkles. And what would you like, Megan?"

"Just plain vanilla in a cup, please," she said as she threw another ball down the alley. She knocked down nine pins and started jumping up and down excitedly.

As I gave my order to the guy behind the

counter (who was the same age as me—I recognized him from school and knew he hung out with the skateboarders), I was able to keep my eye on Tommy and Megan since the concession stand was so close to where we were bowling. First he gave me Megan's cup of vanilla, which I brought over to her.

"Thank you," she said, digging into it with her spoon.

Then I went back for Tommy's vanilla-and-chocolate-swirl cone with sprinkles.

"Here you go!" I said proudly, holding out the cone.

"What's that?" he asked, staring at the cone with a look of disbelief.

"Your ice-cream cone."

He shook his head. "I'm not eating *that*!"

"B-B-But it's what you wanted," I sputtered.

"No, it isn't."

"Yes, it is."

"No, it *isn't*," he stubbornly insisted.

"Tommy, you said you wanted a vanilla-and-chocolate-swirl cone with sprinkles," I explained. "Right?"

"Tommy doesn't like chocolate sprinkles," Megan volunteered. "He only likes rainbow sprinkles."

I looked at the ice-cream cone. It was covered with chocolate sprinkles.

"Chocolate sprinkles are dead ants," Tommy said. "I don't eat ants!"

"But they're *not* ants," I tried to explain. "They're little bits of chocolate. They just *look* like ants."

Tommy tucked in his upper lip and stuck out his lower one. *Nothing* would be getting into that mouth of his.

I looked back and forth between Tommy and Megan. Couldn't one of them have explained the chocolate- versus rainbow-sprinkle rule before I placed the order?

I went back to the counter. "Could I exchange this cone for one with rainbow sprinkles?"

"Yeah, right," the guy laughed, not bothering to look up from the skateboarding magazine he was flipping through. "Ice cream is nonreturnable."

Wise guy!

Before ordering another cone, I double-checked with Tommy to make sure I was getting *exactly* what he wanted—that there was no sugar-cone versus wafer-cone rule that I was unaware of.

"Thank you," he said, taking a bite out of his cone after I'd handed it to him.

Finally, I'd done something right in his eyes!

Now what was I going to do with this other cone? I hated chocolate ice cream but I didn't want to throw the cone out. Then I saw Aaron in the bowling alley's video arcade with Michael. Luckily, Aaron will eat anything.

"Aaron!" I called out. "Aaron!"

My brother came over to our lane. "What do you want?" he asked.

I offered my brother the ice-cream cone.

"What's wrong with it?" he asked suspiciously.

"There's nothing wrong with it," I huffed, shoving it into his hand. "Tommy doesn't like chocolate sprinkles."

"Who's Tommy?" he asked, opening his

mouth wide and inhaling half the cone in one bite, which caused Tommy's mouth to drop open. And promptly want to try the same thing with his cone. Of course, his cone couldn't fit into his tiny mouth and a second later his entire lower face was smeared with vanilla-and-chocolate ice cream and sprinkles.

I pointed to Tommy and Megan as I began cleaning Tommy's face with a napkin. Naturally he started squirming like an eel and wouldn't stand still. "Our new next-door neighbors. I'm babysitting them tonight for their older brother, Kyle."

"Aren't you going to throw a ball, Emma?" Megan asked.

I will be the first to admit that I'm not the world's best bowler. No matter how hard I try, the ball never goes where I want it to. If I throw it to the left, it goes to the right. If I throw it to the right, it goes to the left. If I try to throw a straight ball, it curves. Whenever I bowl, my score is pathetically low, as opposed to my brothers, who are always breaking 200. I'm lucky if my score breaks 100. Even Caitlyn is a better bowler than me!

"I can give you some pointers if you want," Aaron offered.

"Thanks, but we're just messing around."

Aaron shrugged. "Suit yourself," he said, before going back to Michael.

Megan and I played two games (I bowled a 90 and a 75 compared to Megan's 50 and 73. I was on pins and needles our second game. I didn't even want to think how my brothers would tease me if I had been beaten by a seven-year-old!) while Tommy sat watching us, kicking his feet against the floor. Every so often I'd ask him if he wanted to play and every time he said no.

We had just started our third game when Kyle arrived at the alley.

"Kyle!" Tommy and Megan exclaimed happily, running to give him a hug.

Watching Tommy and Megan hug their older brother, I wondered what it would be like to hug him.

Wait a second!

Where had *that* thought suddenly come from?

Well, Kyle certainly *was* huggable. There was no denying that.

And ever since Kyle had moved next door, I found myself thinking of him more and more.

Before I could give it some extra thought, though, Kyle said, "I saw the way you throw your ball."

"And?" I put a hand on my hip and gave him a challenging look. "Think you can do any better?"

"I think I can."

Kyle found a ball that fit. Then he threw it down the alley and got a strike, sending all the pins flying, which caused Tommy to start hooting and hollering. I'd somehow gotten a strike the last game but Tommy hadn't applauded my efforts. *Hmph!*

"Anyone can become a better bowler," Kyle said. "It's just a matter of concentration. See those arrows on the lane?"

"What arrows?"

"Those," Kyle said, pointing them out to me.

"Are they important?"

Kyle stood behind me and slipped my fingers into my ball. Then he lifted my arm up and back in a straight line. "You need to keep your arm straight when you throw your ball. You twist your wrist, which is why your straight ball is never straight. Also, and this is very important, if you focus on a particular arrow when you throw the ball, the ball will go where you want after you release it."

I tried to pay attention to everything Kyle was telling me but I was unable to.

The only thing I was able to focus on was having Kyle so close!

He smelled like soap and summer and coconut and cologne all wrapped up together.

Like most of my friends, I hadn't really started dating yet. But I was definitely wondering what it would be like to have a boyfriend now. I did have some crushes in junior high but that was *junior high*! Guys in junior high are *so* immature. They're more concerned about watching TV and playing video games. But Kyle was different. He seemed older. More confident. Thoughtful, as evidenced by the dinner he'd made for his parents.

And Tommy and Megan both adored him.

Especially Tommy, who had been on his best behavior since Kyle's arrival and was now asking him to show him how to throw a bowling ball.

"Didn't Emma show you, Squirt?"

"Nope," Tommy said, jamming his fingers into a ball that was way too big for his tiny fingers.

Could someone that young be that devious? He wasn't lying but then again, he wasn't exactly telling the truth! How could I show him when he'd refused to let me?

"Let me finish showing Emma how to throw her ball and then I'll show you. Okay?"

Tommy gave Kyle an angelic smile. "Okay."

Oh, the unfairness of it all! This child was no angel!

Kyle explained everything to me again and then told me to try it on my own. Keeping his instructions in mind, I focused on the arrows, concentrating on the one in the middle, and held my arm straight as I released my ball.

It went exactly where I wanted it to.

And I got a strike!

"Yay!" Megan shouted, jumping up and down. "Emma got a strike! Emma got a strike!"

"Big deal," Tommy snorted, still looking for a ball and sticking his fingers into holes. "Kyle got a better strike."

"Your tips really worked!" I exclaimed, giving Kyle a hug, which was the last thing I expected to do.

But once I was into the hug, I went with it.

Other than hugging my dad and my brothers, I'd never really held a guy so close. This was different. I was aware of the hard muscles under his T-shirt as I wrapped my arms around him, pulling him close. And I liked how soft his skin felt as I pulled away after the hug ended, trailing my fingers down his arms.

I liked it a lot.

And I especially liked the fact that while I hugged Kyle, he hugged me back!

But I couldn't really enjoy the moment because just then the Gruesome Twosome arrived, otherwise known as my brothers Aaron and Michael.

"Who's the boy, Em?" Michael asked.

"That's the new guy, Kyle, from next door," Aaron explained. "Hey, Emma, why are you letting *him* give you bowling tips? I offered to help her before but she didn't want my help. Do you *like* Kyle or something?" Aaron began batting his eyelashes and making kissing noises, trying to imitate my voice. "Kiss me, Kyle! Kiss me!"

Foolishly, I thought Michael was going to come to my rescue since he's older and is supposed to be the smarter of the two. Instead, he began singing (with Aaron quickly joining in), "Emma and Kyle sitting in a tree. K-i-s-s-i-n-g."

"KYLE DOESN'T WANT TO KISS EMMA!" Tommy shouted. "SHE'S ICKY!"

I. Was. Going. To. Kill. My. Brothers.

A quick glimpse at Kyle showed that he was blushing red. From embarrassment, I was sure. And I couldn't blame him!

I raced over to Aaron and Michael. "Get.

Out. Of. Here. Now!" I growled between gritted teeth.

"What's that, Em?" Aaron asked, cupping a hand around his ear, pretending to be deaf. "Can't hear you."

"If you value your fingers and ever want to bowl or play a video game again, you will leave *now*!" I repeated.

"Okay! Okay! We get the message!" Michael said. "Sheesh, can't you take a joke?"

"NO!" I hissed.

"She must really like this guy," Aaron said.

Michael grabbed Aaron by the arm. "Come on, let's leave her with her *boyfriend*."

"Bye, Kyle!" Aaron called out in his girly voice, waving good-bye.

Once I saw my brothers walk out of the bowling alley, I turned back to Kyle, who was no longer blushing. Had he heard what Aaron said? About me liking him? I hoped not. Because I *did* like him but not *like* him *like* him. The way you did a boyfriend. I liked him as a friend.

Didn't I?

Or did I like him like a possible boyfriend?

"Sorry about that," I apologized, deciding I'd sort through my feelings later. "Sometimes older brothers can be jerks."

"Take that back!" Tommy demanded. "My older brother isn't a jerk!"

"Emma wasn't talking about me, Squirt," Kyle explained, running a hand over Tommy's hair. "Go check out that blue ball. I think it might fit your fingers." Kyle turned back to me as Tommy ran off. "Don't worry about it. They were just playing around."

And spoiling what could have been a nice moment between us, I thought.

We played one more game and Tommy even cheered for me when I got a spare. Of course, he forgot all about that when we were walking home and I offered him my hand to hold on to. Instead, he ran ahead with Megan.

"Can I ask you something?" Kyle said.

"You need me to babysit again?" I joked. "Tonight was a freebie, but the next time is going to cost you."

"Are you doing anything on Saturday?"

Saturday? Why was Kyle asking me about Saturday?

Saturday was usually date night.

He wasn't . . .

Was he?!

I tried to sound cool and collected as I pretended to think. "Saturday. Hmmm. No. I don't have any plans on Saturday. Day or night. Why?"

"On my way over to the bowling alley I saw a poster for the county fair. Would you like to go with me Saturday afternoon?"

I started to feel all warm and fuzzy inside. Kyle was asking me out!

"As a way of thanking you for all your hard work today," he quickly stated.

Oh.

I was no longer feeling warm and fuzzy.

"Just you and me? Or will we be having company?" I asked, nodding at Megan and Tommy.

"Just you and me."

Okay, so it wasn't a date.

But . . .

It *was* an afternoon *alone* with Kyle.

My mind was instantly made up.

"I'd love to!"

Chapter Seven

The first thing I did when I got home was call Caitlyn. Or at least I tried to, but her line was busy, which meant she was online. So I sent her an instant message and told her to call me.

My phone rang a minute later.

"What's up?" she asked.

"Guess who I'm going to the county fair with on Saturday?"

"I dunno. Who? Joey Harris? Matthew Chin? Lucas Fiori? If it's any of them, you've hit the jackpot. They're all cuties."

"Caitlyn!" I wailed. "Come on! Think!"

"It's not Joey, Matt, or Luke? Huh. You've got me stumped. Unless it's someone new." Caitlyn paused. "Someone new . . . you don't mean?" She gasped. "The boy next door? What's his name again? Kyle?"

"Yes!" I squealed excitedly.

"You go, girl!"

"But it's not a date," I quickly clarified.

"What do you mean?"

"He's just thanking me for the way I helped him out today."

"What'd you do?"

I quickly filled Caitlyn in on Kyle's kitchen disaster and my babysitting duties. "He asked me when we were walking home from the bowling alley."

"Was it a romantic walk? Were you holding hands? Did he try to kiss you? Details! I want details!"

"It was *not* a romantic walk. How romantic could it be? We were chaperoning his seven-year-old sister and five-year-old brother."

"Bummer. But you'd like things to go in that

direction, right? Come on, Emma. Don't lie to me. I'm your best friend. I can always tell when you're holding back."

That was true. Whenever I had a crush on someone, I kept it to myself. It was like I was afraid to tell anyone else because if I did, I would jinx myself and then that guy wouldn't like me.

"Remember in fifth grade when we had Secret Santas?" Caitlyn said. "I'd picked Andy Wallace's name and you had Gus Winthrop and you *begged* me to give you Andy so you could be his Secret Santa. And I wouldn't give you his name until you fessed up that you liked him."

"For two weeks I left Christmas cookies and candy canes in his desk," I grumbled. "And when he found out I was his Secret Santa, he complained! He said he didn't like sugar cookies and if I ever brought him cookies again, to make sure they were chocolate chip."

"Loser!" Caitlyn sang. "So, spill! Do you like this guy?"

"Yes, I like him," I confessed. "But I'm not sure if he likes me."

"That's easy enough to fix."

"It is?"

"Of course! We'll make sure you look fabulous on Saturday. Like that scene in *Grease* when Sandy has her makeover, and Danny turns into a drooling slob when he sees her for the first time. Do you know what you're going to wear?"

"No!" I admitted, suddenly panicked. I hadn't even thought of my clothes. What was I going to wear?!

"Calm down! You've got a closet full of great things. We'll come up with something cute. You've got that adorable peach top with the puffy sleeves. Oooh, and then there's that violet sundress with the halter neck. The outfit will be easy, but what about your hair? Are you going to wear it loose? French braid? Ponytail? Curled?"

My head was spinning as Caitlyn kept talking nonstop. "I can't do this all myself. You're going to have to sleep over on Friday night."

I expected her to instantly say yes, the way she always did. Instead, Caitlyn slowly said, "I can't sleep over."

"How come? Are you going out of town with your family?"

"No-o-o-o."

I was confused. "Then why can't you sleep over?"

"I just can't."

"Caitlyn!"

"Emma!"

"Tell me!" I insisted.

"It's Aaron!" she whispered, as if she was afraid my brother might overhear her. "He'll see me in the morning."

"So?" I didn't get what the problem was. "He's seen you in the morning hundreds of times."

"You know how bad I look in the morning. My hair is always a frizzy mess. And what if he talks to me before I've brushed my teeth? Ick!"

Aaron? Talk to Caitlyn in the morning? I'm lucky if he even talks to me! And I'm his sister!

"You can't be serious."

"I am."

"Caitlyn, I need you! You can't abandon me!" It was time for the guilt. "Who watched your cat in January when you had to go on that ski trip with your father's company? And who babysat your cousin Ira in April when you had that family wedding and your aunt couldn't get her regular babysitter?"

"You were paid!" Caitlyn reminded.

"But I had to change his diaper *three* times and every time he'd done number two!"

"Okay, okay, fine," she grumbled. "I'll sleep over. But I'm not leaving your bedroom on Saturday morning until I look decent. Deal?"

"Deal!"

After getting off the phone with Caitlyn, I spent some time online, popping onto some of my favorite websites. Then I decided to check my email account at school. There had been that one email from Romeo. Maybe someone else had decided to turn to Daisy for advice.

My in-box had another email in it.

And it was from Romeo again!

What could he be writing to me about this time?

I quickly opened his email and started reading.

Dear Daisy: Remember that girl I
wrote to you about? She's still around. I
decided to give her a second chance.

That was it? He didn't have anything else to
tell me? How could he leave me hanging this
way? I checked the time he'd sent the email.
Only ten minutes earlier. Hmmm. Maybe he
was still online. I had to know what was going
on with him and this girl. I quickly sent off a
reply.

And?

A while passed and then there was a *ding*.
I had mail!

And I can't figure her out. It's like she's got
two sides to her personality. Some days
she's really sweet and other days she's
really crazy. I never know what to expect
when I'm around her. What's your advice?

This was a no-brainer!

Dear Romeo: Some girls can be like the weather. Totally unpredictable. Calm and sunny one day. Then dark and stormy the next. We're not all this way—I'm certainly not, just fyi—but trust me, a lot of us are. And she sounds like one of them. My advice to you? Steer clear! This girl sounds like one twisted sister! xoxox, Daisy

I waited for Romeo to write back, but he didn't. Maybe he didn't like what I had to say. I'd certainly given him something to think about.

After I logged off, I couldn't stop thinking about Romeo. Obviously he liked this girl he was writing about. So much so that he wasn't willing to give up on her. I didn't know him, but I felt that he deserved better. Who wanted an unpredictable girlfriend? Hopefully he'd follow my advice.

Otherwise, chances were the next time he wrote in, he'd be telling me about his broken heart.

I wondered why I was worrying about

Romeo's love life. I had my own to worry about!

And the only way I was going to figure out if I *did* have a love life was this Saturday at the county fair.

With that thought in mind, I headed straight for my closet and started going through my outfits.

Chapter Eight

"How about this?" Caitlyn asked.

I looked up from my bed, where I was flipping through the newest issue of *People*. Lindsay Lohan was on the cover with the headline: HE BROKE MY HEART! It looked like Lindsay's latest romance was over. What was this for her? Boyfriend Number Five so far this year? I hadn't even had Boyfriend Number One yet!

Caitlyn was holding up a white pleated miniskirt and a short-sleeved aquamarine top. I made a face. "I wore that to the class picnic, remember?"

"Yes, I remember. And everyone said you looked great! So why not stick with something that's worked?"

"I want to wear something different."

Caitlyn pulled out a pink baby tee that said 100% NATURAL and a pair of white shorts. "How about this?"

"Too casual," I said, barely looking up from the magazine.

She pulled out a lime-green sundress decorated with daisies. "This?"

"Too dressy."

Caitlyn threw up her hands. "I give up!" She sighed in exasperation and flopped down next to me on my bed, yanking my copy of *People* out of my hands and tossing it to the floor. "Why aren't you putting any effort into this? You always love deciding what you're going to wear."

I shrugged. "I don't know."

Caitlyn looked directly into my eyes. "What's wrong? You seem down."

She was right. That's why she was my best

friend. She always knew when something was wrong. Like in fifth grade, when I had the lead in the school play. The night before my first performance, I was a nervous wreck. I couldn't remember half of my lines. But Caitlyn, who had called me on the phone to wish me luck, could hear something in my voice. And when I finally told her I was scared, she told me I was going to be great and that she would be sitting right in the first row, rooting for me.

She was.

And I didn't forget a single line.

Maybe it would be good to talk about what was bothering me. Maybe it could help me figure things out.

"I haven't seen Kyle at all this week," I said.

Caitlyn looked perplexed. "And that's a problem because . . . ?"

"Because I've been hoping our going out together would turn into a date. I was hoping he liked me," I admitted, wondering if I was jinxing myself, saying out loud that I liked Kyle. "If you like someone, you want to be around them as much as possible, right? You want them to *know* that you like them, right? Even if they're maybe too shy to say it. Sometimes actions speak louder than words."

Caitlyn nodded. "That makes sense."

"But I haven't seen him *at all* this week! It's like he's the Invisible Man! And if he hasn't been hanging around me, well, I guess that means he doesn't like me the way I like him."

"Not necessarily," Caitlyn said. "He's probably been busy. Remember, he and his family just moved in. I'm sure they're still unpacking. And he does have a little brother and sister. I'll bet he's busy with them, too. You know, babysitting them during the day while his parents are at work."

"So what about at night when his parents are home and he has free time?" I countered.

Caitlyn shrugged. "He's probably out exploring. Hanging out at the mall. Going to the arcade. Maybe tossing a few hoops at the basketball court. You're overreacting, Em. You know how guys are. He asked you to the fair and he's not even going to think about it until Saturday."

"I suppose you could be right," I grudgingly admitted, starting to feel a spark of hope. Maybe I was jumping to conclusions. Maybe Kyle *did* like me. Maybe . . .

"Or maybe *you're* right," Caitlyn said, breaking into my thoughts.

"What?!" I exclaimed in shock.

"Just hear me out," she said gently, placing a hand on my arm. "Maybe he does just want to thank you. But you can change his mind after the two of you spend the day together. I mean, so far, you haven't really spent a lot of time with him."

"No, but he's always seen me at my worst!" I wailed, burying my face in my pillow.

"That's why we have to make sure you look your best!" Caitlyn exclaimed, jumping off my bed, grabbing me by the hand, and dragging me to my closet.

"Why can't I be a mind reader so I can see what he's thinking?"

"Just be yourself," Caitlyn said. "That's the best advice I can give."

I nodded. "You're right. But I'm going to

be so nervous!"

"Would it help if you had some support?" Caitlyn asked as she began searching through my hangers.

I gave Caitlyn a puzzled look. "What do you mean?"

"Why don't we double-date?"

"Someone asked you out and you didn't tell me until *now*?!" I shrieked. "Who is it? Who? Who? Who? Tell me who it is!"

"He hasn't asked me out. *Yet*," Caitlyn admitted. "But maybe if we said something to Aaron . . ."

Aaron?! I should have known!

"No, no, no!" I groaned.

"Yes, yes, yes! Come on, Em. Pleeease! I'll be your best friend."

"You already are my best friend," I reminded her.

"I'll be your best friend forever," she said.

"*Why* do you want to go out with Aaron?" I asked. "I don't get it!"

"He's cute," Caitlyn said, blushing.

As much as I hate to admit it, Aaron *is* cute.

I mean, for a jerky brother. And he does have a certain puppy-dog charm. Big brown eyes. A mop of messy brown hair. Dimples that pop out whenever he smiles. But those looks were deceptive. They masked his inner evil!

"He used to torture us when we were little," I reminded Caitlyn. "He still tortures me! I told you what he and Michael did to me at the bowling alley." I gasped. "That's it!"

"What?"

"That's why Kyle hasn't been around!" Why hadn't I realized it sooner? "Because of my stupid brothers! He probably thinks if they see us together, they'll start teasing us. He said their teasing didn't bother him, but maybe it did!"

"So I guess that means you don't want to double-date with Aaron," Caitlyn said glumly.

"Double-dating with Aaron would be a disaster," I said. "But that doesn't mean you can't go to the fair with him. If you like Aaron, you should just tell him."

Caitlyn gave me a horrified look. "I can't!"

"Then he's never going to know you like

him." An idea popped into my head. "You know, Caitlyn. Sometimes you have to sink or swim."

"What are you talking about?"

I grabbed her by the hand and dragged her out of my bedroom. "Come on!"

"Where are we going?"

"To the family room," I said. "We'll figure out what I'm going to wear later. Right now, we're going to let Aaron know that you like him!"

Getting Caitlyn downstairs was a battle. As soon as she heard that I planned to tell Aaron that she had a crush on him, she grabbed on to the banister at the top of the stairs and wouldn't let go. Finally, I agreed that I wouldn't say anything to Aaron if she agreed to come with me to the family room.

"You like being around him, right?"

"Yes," she admitted, still refusing to let go of the banister.

"Then we'll hang out with him. See what he's watching on TV. Maybe it'll give the two of you something to talk about. And that could lead to other topics. Who knows? You both might have a lot in common."

Caitlyn eyed me suspiciously. "You promise not to tell him I like him?"

I sighed. "I promise," I said, crossing my heart. Of course I wasn't going to say anything to Aaron. I wouldn't be that mean! But I was hoping Caitlyn would think I would and tell him herself. "But if you like him, I want to try to help him realize that someone special is right under his nose. Is that okay?"

"Yes," she said, letting go of the banister. "But remember! You can't tell him I like him!"

"My lips are sealed!"

When we arrived in the family room, all my thoughts of playing matchmaker for Caitlyn disappeared when I saw who was sitting on the couch with my brothers.

Kyle.

I was speechless.

So much for my theory that he was afraid of my brothers teasing him! He and Aaron and Michael were talking nonstop, laughing and playfully shoving one another.

At first I just stood there, not knowing what to say. Then Caitlyn elbowed me in the side and I found my voice.

"Kyle!" I exclaimed, giving him a smile. "What are you doing here?"

"I ran into Aaron when I was riding my bike and he invited me over."

"We're going to watch some movies," Michael said, slipping a disk into the DVD player.

"What are you going to watch?" Caitlyn asked.

"Horror movies," Aaron said.

Caitlyn squealed. "Ick! I hate horror movies."

So did I. All that blood. All that screaming. And never knowing when the killer was going to jump out and scare you! I'll take a nice romantic comedy like *Clueless* or *Legally Blond* any day.

"No one says you have to stay and watch," Aaron said, reaching into a bowl of popcorn, his eyes glued to the TV screen.

"Don't hog it all!" Michael shouted, grabbing the bowl out of his hands and lying down on the rug.

"Emma and I didn't have any plans," Caitlyn said, taking Michael's empty seat next to Aaron. "We'll stay. Okay with you, Em?"

Even though I hated horror movies, this was a chance to spend some time with Kyle and I wasn't going to pass it up!

"Sure," I said. "Caitlyn, this is Kyle, our new neighbor," I introduced, pretending she didn't know who he was. "Kyle, this is my best friend, Caitlyn."

"Caitlyn practically lives here," Aaron said as the movie started and creepy horror music filled the room. "It's like having two sisters."

Caitlyn gave me a panicked look. That was *so* not what she wanted to hear!

I shrugged. My big brother was clueless. Unless someone told him that Caitlyn liked him, he wasn't going to think of her as possible girlfriend material.

"Hey, Em, turn off the light, would you?"

Michael asked.

I turned off the overhead light and took the empty seat next to Kyle. It wasn't a tight fit, but I was sitting close enough next to him that our arms were touching. It was like static electricity! I actually shivered! And when I did, our arms bumped against each other some more. I started pondering how I could "accidentally" brush my arm against his again. Maybe . . .

Hey!

Wait a minute!

Kyle had scootched away from me!

We'd been sitting elbow to elbow and now there was a space between us!

I looked across at Caitlyn, who was purposely not looking at the TV screen. I didn't blame her. A hockey mask–wearing maniac was waving a bloody chain saw in the air. Ugh!

"I'm going to get a soda," I said. "Anyone want anything?"

"Scared already, Em?" Aaron teased. "Better watch out or the boogeyman is gonna getcha!"

I rolled my eyes. "Real mature, Aaron."

I headed into the kitchen and Caitlyn quickly followed.

"What was up with the scootch?" Caitlyn asked before I could say anything.

"You saw it too!" I gasped, opening up a can of root beer and taking a sip. "Then it wasn't my imagination!"

Caitlyn shook her head. "Nope."

"Is it my breath?" I asked, breathing into the palm of my hand. "We had hamburgers for dinner tonight but mine didn't have any onions."

"Let me get a whiff," Caitlyn said, sticking her face in front of my mouth and sniffing. "Minty fresh and a little root beery, but that's it."

I sniffed under my arms, almost afraid to ask the question. "Do I have BO?"

Caitlyn walked around me, sniffing closely. "All I smell is Coast soap, Downy fabric softener, and Sarah Jessica Parker's Lovely perfume."

"Then what's the problem?" I asked.

Caitlyn shrugged. "He's a guy. Who can figure them out?"

I should, I thought to myself in frustration. *After all, I'm Dear Daisy!*

Come on, Emma! I scolded myself. *Think! Why would Kyle scootch away from you?*

What possible reason could there be?

Unless . . .

Unless he didn't want my brothers to see how close we were sitting together. That could be why he'd scootched. . . .

"Should we head back out there?" Caitlyn asked, shivering as we heard a scream come from the TV.

"No way," I said, starting to open up the kitchen cabinets, looking for the ingredients to make chocolate chip cookies.

By the time the cookies were ready, the movie was over. Caitlyn and I both went out to the family room with a big heaping plate of cookies.

"Anyone in the mood for cookies?" I asked.

Aaron and Michael instantly grabbed a handful of cookies from Caitlyn's plate. No surprise there. They acted like they hadn't eaten in weeks.

"How about you, Kyle?" I asked, holding out my plate to him.

"No thanks."

"Are you sure?"

"Yeah."

"How was the movie?"

"Okay."

"Were you scared? Even though I know it's all fake, I still get scared."

"No."

"I haven't seen you all week," I said. "Where've you been?"

"Around."

I wanted to scream! What was with the one-word answers? It was like Kyle didn't want to talk to me. Had I done something to offend him?

"Hey, Emma, do you mind if we talk alone?" he asked.

I scolded myself for once again jumping to conclusions. He was shy. That's all it was! He didn't want everyone else hearing what he had to say to me. Luckily, my brothers had started playing a video game. "Sure."

"Why don't we go out on the front porch?" he suggested.

Oooh! He wanted privacy!

Privacy meant romance!

Caitlyn heard Kyle ask me to go out on the front porch and clapped her hands happily as I followed him out of the family room.

We went outside and I sat next to Kyle on our hanging porch swing, which was made of white wicker. The smell of freshly cut grass was still thick in the air from when Aaron had mowed the lawn earlier that night, along with the scent of my mother's blooming roses in the front yard. There was a slight breeze and a full moon up in the sky. It was the perfect summer night. I felt this sudden surge of happiness. Anything seemed possible. It was summer — the time for romance!

I wondered what Kyle wanted to talk to me about. He looked so serious! Like he didn't know what he was supposed to do next. He was sitting at the far end of the swing. All stiff. Why didn't he have his arm casually tossed on the back of the swing? That way when I sat next to him, he could then "casually" move his arm from the back of the swing to my shoulders.

Unless . . .

Maybe he was going to take me into his arms.

Maybe he was going to give me my first kiss!

I decided to sit next to him and see what would happen. I kept waiting for him to make a move, but he didn't. We sat next to each other in silence until finally I turned to him and asked, "What did you want to talk to me about?"

"I'm sorry this is so last minute but I can't take you to the county fair tomorrow," he said, not looking directly at me. It was like he was nervous. He was chewing his lower lip and his eyes kept wandering around, looking at anything but me. Almost like he didn't want to face me. "Something's suddenly come up."

My mouth dropped open. Those were the last words I'd been expecting to hear.

I wanted to say something, but couldn't. I didn't know what to say.

"Emma? Are you okay?"

No, I was *not* okay. I was *majorly* disappointed! But it was my own fault. I'd built up a fantasy in my head, thinking that Kyle and I would go to the fair together and somehow, some way, our afternoon out as friends would turn into a romantic date.

I finally found my voice.

"It's no big deal," I said, trying to sound cheery. Calm. *Not* upset. Trying to sound like it didn't bother me. But it *did*, all right. "These things happen. We'll hang out together another time."

"Absolutely," Kyle agreed, suddenly looking relieved. Like a huge weight had been lifted off his shoulders. "Because I owe you for helping me out."

He *owed* me? *Owed me?!* That didn't sound the least bit romantic!

"I better get home," Kyle said, getting off the swing. "I'll see you around."

"See ya," I said, watching as he walked across our front lawn to his house.

When I went back inside, I found Caitlyn

waiting by the front door. She instantly pounced on me, grabbing my arm and dragging me upstairs to my room.

"Spill, spill, spill!" she cried once my bedroom door was closed, the better to keep out eavesdropping brothers. "My love life might be fizzling but yours is *sizzling*!"

"Mine's fizzling too," I said.

"What?"

"Kyle can't take me to the fair tomorrow," I announced. I felt completely defeated.

Shock washed over Caitlyn's face. "He broke your date?"

"It wasn't a date," I reminded her miserably.

"What happened?"

"He said something suddenly came up."

"What was the *something* that came up?" she asked.

I shrugged. "I don't know. I didn't ask."

"You didn't ask?"

"No, I didn't!" I snapped, letting out all the feelings I'd been keeping bottled up inside. "He caught me completely off guard. The last thing I thought he was going to say was that he couldn't take me to the fair. I was expecting a kiss. Not a kiss-off!"

"Well, it really wasn't a date," Caitlyn said.

I knew she was trying to make me feel better. Even though it hadn't officially been a date, I'd been thinking of it as one. Part of me wanted to cry, and part of me just felt so stupid!

"Are you disappointed?" she asked.

"Yes. No. I don't know. I haven't felt this way since that crazy crush on Jackson Moore in seventh grade. But this felt different."

"How?"

"I can't explain it. I guess there was actually hope that he'd like me back . . . I mean, it's not just that he's cute. He's so sweet with his family! Plus, he's smart and wants to be an artist. I don't know, it's more than that. Like there's something in the air between us. But I just can't tell how he feels!"

Caitlyn snapped her fingers. "I know what you should do!"

"What?"

"You should send an email to Dear Daisy."

I gulped. "Dear Daisy?"

"She's always giving out advice when people write in to her about their love problems."

"I don't know, Caitlyn."

I couldn't tell Caitlyn that Daisy wouldn't be able to help me because *I* was Daisy. But she could see that I was upset and she wanted to help me feel better. I couldn't deny her that.

"What do you have to lose?" she asked.

I sighed. "Okay, I'll send an email to Daisy."

With Caitlyn looking over my shoulder, I typed out an email to Daisy. I decided to keep it short and sweet.

Dear Daisy: There's this boy that I like a lot but I don't know if he likes me. Any advice?

"She'll tell you what to do," Caitlyn stated confidently after I'd sent the email. "She's such a love expert. She probably has guys calling her all the time!"

Yeah, right! I thought.

Chapter Nine

"Let's check to see if Daisy wrote back to you!"

I groaned, burying my head under my pillow as bright morning sunshine filled my bedroom. I am *not* a morning person. Caitlyn, on the other hand, always wakes up early, no matter what time she goes to bed. Last night after we emailed Daisy, we stayed in my room and watched a *My Super Sweet Sixteen* marathon on MTV, screaming at the TV the entire time because we hated every girl in every episode. Talk about selfish monsters! When we couldn't stand watching them anymore, we listened to CDs while flipping through magazines, talking about when we would turn sixteen and what kind of parties we wanted to have. We finally went to sleep at three A.M.

I snuck a peek at my clock radio. It was nine A.M.

"Caitlyn, it's too early to get up," I said, pulling the sheets over my head. I needed *at least* two more hours of beauty sleep!

"It is not!" she insisted, pulling the sheets off me. "We've got a lot to do today!"

"Like what?" I grumbled. "I'm dateless, remember? Not that I really had a date to begin with."

"That doesn't mean we can't still go to the fair and have a good time."

"I suppose."

"So Kyle's not interested. Fine. His loss. That doesn't mean some other cute guy isn't going to want to go out with you."

But I don't want to go out with some other guy. I want to go out with Kyle!

I opened up one eye, realizing I could stay in

bed feeling sorry for myself or I could follow Caitlyn's advice. "What time do you want to go?"

"That's the spirit!" Caitlyn pulled me out of bed. "But first let's check your email."

I knew there wouldn't be an email waiting from Daisy, but I couldn't tell Caitlyn that it was because *I* was Daisy and I hadn't written to myself. When we checked my email account, the email Caitlyn was expecting wasn't there.

"She didn't write back," Caitlyn said with disappointment.

"Maybe she hasn't checked her email yet. Or she could be away."

"I guess."

"Why don't you take a shower first?" I suggested.

"Are you sure it's safe for me to use the bathroom?" Caitlyn asked, sticking her head out into the hallway and looking to the left and right. "I'm not going to run into Aaron, am I?"

"Aaron doesn't get up until at least twelve on a Saturday. You're safe. Trust me."

"Okay," Caitlyn said, tiptoeing out of my bedroom and past Aaron's closed door.

After Caitlyn left I decided to log on to Daisy's account. I had a plan. I was going to send an email to myself and then tell Caitlyn that "Daisy" had written back.

But my plan was forgotten when I logged on to Daisy's account and saw that in addition to the email I had sent last night, there was another one waiting.

And it was from Romeo!

I instantly opened it up, wondering what he had to say.

> Dear Daisy: Well, I followed your advice.
> But guess what? I can't stop thinking about
> this girl. That must mean something, right?
> What should I do, Daisy? Make a move or
> just move on? Romeo

I could hear the shower running in the background. I had some time, but not much. Caitlyn would be back soon. My fingers flew over my keyboard.

> Dear Romeo: Everyone thinks I have the

answers when it comes to love, but I really
don't. The advice I gave you last time was
wrong. Obviously it's not working if you're
still into this girl. I don't know you and I
don't know her. But maybe there's a reason she's acting so crazy. If you really like
her, you should go after her. Give her
another chance. Sometimes, when it
comes to love, you have to fight for it.
xoxox, Daisy

After I sent the email and logged off, I felt
like a huge load had been lifted off my shoulders. Suddenly, I no longer felt sorry for
myself. I wasn't the only one who couldn't figure things out when it came to love. But hopefully I'd helped Romeo straighten out his love
life. And that gave me a good feeling.

What didn't give me a good feeling was all
the bright sunshine flooding into my bedroom.
It was too intense and my room was getting
hot. I needed to pull down the shades. As I
walked over to the window, I caught a glimpse
of Kyle outside of his house. I was going to call

out a hello when I noticed that he wasn't alone.

And what I saw next caused me to do a double take.

Kyle was wrapping his arm around the shoulders of a beautiful redhead!

Was Ravishing Red the "something" that had "suddenly" come up?

I pressed myself against the side of my window, not wanting to be seen, but not wanting to miss any of what was going on outside.

Just then Caitlyn came back into my room. She was in a white terry cloth robe, drying her hair with a fluffy blue towel. "What are you doing?" she asked. "You look like you're spying on someone."

"I am!"

"You are? Who?"

"Kyle!" I pointed to the other side of the window. "Take a look."

Caitlyn raced over to the wall next to the window and pressed herself against it. Then she quickly ducked her head to the side and looked outside. When she ducked back, her mouth was wide open.

I took another peek out the window, watching as Kyle and Red walked down the block. His arm was still around her and they were talking and laughing, Red playfully punching Kyle on his shoulder.

Only one thought was going through my mind.

Who was this girl?!

Chapter Ten

"So who do you think she is?" Caitlyn asked.

"I don't know," I answered.

We were in the backseat of my brother Rob's car, getting driven to the county fair. For once the car was clean and odor free. That's because sitting next to Rob in the front seat was his girlfriend Cathy, and after a year of dating her, he knew Cathy wouldn't put up with a stinky, messy car. She lived one town over from ours and they'd met at college during freshman orientation last September. I liked

Cathy a lot. She was a petite brunette who wore her hair in a short pixie cut and had the most beautiful violet-blue eyes I'd ever seen. Not only was she pretty and smart (she planned on being a doctor) but she didn't take any crap from my brother. I liked that the most.

"Do you think Ravishing Red is the reason why you haven't seen Kyle all week?" Cathy asked.

I had given Cathy a quick summary of the Kyle situation once we'd hit the road and then told her of the latest development.

I shrugged. "I don't know. Maybe."

"How pretty was she?" Cathy asked.

"Very," Caitlyn and I both answered at once.

"If you want my advice, move on," Cathy said. "There are plenty of other guys out there."

"Hey!" Rob exclaimed as he stopped for a red light. "That's my baby sister you're talking to. She's not ready to date yet."

I loved when Rob got into overprotective mode. It showed me that deep down he cared.

"Kyle gives you any trouble, you just let me

know and I'll have a little *talk* with him." Rob smacked a fist into the palm of his hand. "If you know what I mean."

Yikes! I didn't want poor Kyle to get a pounding just because he didn't like me. We weren't even dating!

"I don't think you'll have to do that," I said, as the light turned green and Rob started driving again.

"I didn't recognize her from school," Caitlyn said. "Did you?"

I shook my head. "I never saw her before in my life. Maybe she's new. Like Kyle."

"And that's what drew them together," Caitlyn gushed. "New boy falls in love with new girl. It's just like the plot of a Lindsay Lohan movie."

"I think the way she looks also had something to do with it," I said drily. Ravishing Red was *gorgeous*. "What guy could resist *that*?!"

"Not all guys are just obsessed with looks," Rob said. "Anyway, you're doing fine in the looks department yourself. So don't worry about this guy. He must be a loser if he's not into you."

Awww! I was *loving* my big brother today! If he wasn't busy driving, I'd have thrown my arms around him in a hug.

"I love what you're wearing," Cathy said to me.

I had decided I wasn't going to let Kyle and the Mystery of Ravishing Red get me down. It was a super-sunny summer day and I was going to dress that way. I'd chosen a pair of yellow capri pants from American Eagle, an off-the-shoulder white shirt, and a pair of white satin sandals with a slightly high heel. The sandals were the best part. My aunt Martha had bought them for me in SoHo when I'd visited her in New York City last spring. They were the most expensive shoes I'd ever owned!

To top it all off, I wore a pair of sunburst-shaped earrings, a couple of bangle bracelets, and my hair was loose.

Caitlyn had gone with the summer theme as well. She was wearing a Gap jean skirt with a hot pink halter top and pink slides (I suspected she'd "borrowed" the shoes from her sister, Tess—Caitlyn *always* borrowed from Tess without asking, which always led to huge screaming matches—because the heels were *very* high and I'd never seen Caitlyn wear them before).

"Are you going to be able to walk in those things?" I asked Caitlyn, remembering how she'd wobbled to the car.

"Yes," she said, although she didn't sound certain.

"The guys are definitely going to notice both of you," Cathy said.

"Enough with the guy talk!" Rob barked as we reached the fair and he started looking for a parking space.

"I'm just going to have a good time today," I told Cathy. "Go on the rides. Eat some hot dogs and cotton candy. Maybe win a couple of prizes."

"You've got it bad for him, huh?" Cathy said knowingly.

Did I? I really didn't know. Seeing Kyle with Ravishing Red had been a bit of a shock. After the shock came the hurt. Why was he with her and not me? I liked him and I wanted him to like me. But you can't "make" someone like you.

What did you do when you liked someone and they didn't like you back?

Why was I even asking myself that question? I scolded myself. I knew the answer. You move on.

"I'm going to give you one last bit of advice," Cathy said. "Guys who two-time are jerks. Steer clear of them. Once a cheater, always a cheater. I wouldn't put up with any of that."

"Why do I have a feeling you're directing that comment to me?" Rob asked as he turned off the car.

Cathy kissed him on the cheek. "Just wanted to make sure you were listening, sweetie."

Even though we got to the fair early, it was mobbed. We left Rob and Cathy and went to check out the games first. We tried to throw basketballs through hoops, squirted water guns into balloons, and threw baseballs at empty soda cans. Each and every time, we lost.

"I want to win one of those Kewpie dolls," Caitlyn said.

"You've already spent five dollars trying to toss hoops over those square blocks. It's impossible."

"No, it's not," Caitlyn insisted. "It's just a matter of concentration. If I concentrate—" The rest of the words died in her throat as she grabbed my arm. "I think I just saw Aaron!"

All thoughts of Kewpie dolls were instantly forgotten.

"How do I look?" she asked, combing her hair with her fingers.

"Sensational," I said.

"I'm going to go find him," she said, popping a stick of Dentyne into her mouth. "Maybe I can get him to win me the Kewpie doll. Guys love a challenge!"

And with that she went wobbling off on her high heels, leaving me alone.

Hmph! Abandoned for a guy! And not just any guy, but my annoying older brother! Where did this fall in the "Best Friends

Handbook"?

I wasn't alone for long. Seconds after Caitlyn disappeared into the crowd my friend Gwen came running up to me.

Gwen is gorgeous and I totally admire her sense of style. Her skin is the color of cocoa and she wears her light brown hair in loose curls. And like me, she loves clothes! Today she was wearing white shorts, a beaded tank top I'd seen at Abercrombie a week ago, and the most adorable wedges decorated with tiny turquoise stones. No matter what she wears, she makes it look like she just threw it on. So natural. I totally envy her that.

"Emma! You've got to help me!"

"What's up?"

"I've been working the charity dunking booth but there's a crisis at the pie-eating table. All the pies that we ordered haven't shown up and I need to call the bakery. If they haven't delivered them, I'm going to have to find someone to take me to the bakery. Could you take over for me at the dunking booth? I shouldn't be gone long. An hour, tops."

"Sure." That was another thing about Gwen. She was always volunteering for everything. It would have been way too selfish to say no. Besides, how hard could it be selling balls to throw?

Gwen gave me a hug. "You're a lifesaver! I owe you big-time! The booth is all the way at the end." She pointed with her finger. "Coach Morrison is there."

I shooed Gwen away. "Go take care of your pies. I'll take care of the dunking booth."

I found Coach Morrison waiting for me at the booth. I knew who he was because he had coached all my brothers. He was an older man in his fifties with a gray buzz cut and lots of muscles. Before becoming a high school coach, he'd been a sergeant in the army.

"Reporting for duty," I said, giving him a tiny salute.

"Just climb up the ladder and sit on the plank," he instructed.

I looked at him in confusion. "Huh?"

"Climb up the ladder and sit on the plank," he repeated, this time more slowly.

"Why?" I asked, still not understanding his instructions. Why did he want me to sit on that high plank above that vat of water?

"So this line of people can try to dunk you!"

Wait. *I* was the girl who was going to get dunked?

What?!

This wasn't what I'd signed on for!

I could see a line was already forming. Guys waiting to put down their money for the chance to dunk me!

I pulled Coach Morrison to one side. "Couldn't we switch?" I suggested. "I'll sell the balls and you sit on the plank?"

He pointed to the sign next to the booth. It said DUNK THE LOVELY LADY.

"Do I look like a lovely lady?" he asked.

I sighed.

He pointed to the ladder. "Up!"

I couldn't let Gwen down. I had promised to fill in for her, and it *was* for charity. It was my own fault for not asking her *exactly* what I'd be doing.

"Don't be scared," Coach Morrison said. "If

it makes you feel any better, Gwen was sitting up there for three hours and she didn't get dunked once. None of these guys can throw to save their life. When you come back down you'll be as dry as when you went up."

That made me feel a little bit better, but not much.

Reluctantly, I climbed up the ladder and sat in the center of the plank. Looking down, I could see the crystal-clear blue water in the vat below me.

It's only for an hour, I reminded myself. *Only for an hour. And Coach Morrison said Gwen had been sitting up here for three hours and she wasn't dunked once.*

"Step right up, folks! Step right up!" Coach Morrison began shouting like a carnival barker. "See if you can dunk the pretty girl! One dollar will get you three balls. Step right up!"

As Coach Morrison had predicted, none of the guys could throw to save their life. Their balls didn't come anywhere near the bull's-eye they needed to hit in order to dunk me. And it wasn't so bad sitting up here. The weather had cooled off a bit. There was a nice breeze and I could see the entire fair.

I checked the time on my watch. An hour had gone by. Hopefully Gwen would be on her way back and I could go back to enjoying the fair. My stomach had started rumbling a few seconds earlier. Maybe I'd buy a hot dog with lots of relish and sauerkraut. And a nice icy Coke. That would really hit the spot.

"Helloooo, Emma!"

Thoughts of lunch were forgotten as I gazed down and saw who was handing his money to Coach Morrison.

Oh no!

No!

Nooo!!!!!

Standing at the counter, buying *six* base-balls, was my brother Aaron.

And standing behind him, also with his money out, was my brother Michael.

"You wouldn't dare!" I hissed.

"Why not?" Michael asked. "It's for char-ity."

What could I say to that? He was right.

"Don't worry, Em!" Aaron said, getting ready to throw his first ball. "It'll be over before you know it."

Aaron threw his first ball and I braced myself to get dunked.

But I didn't.

He missed.

The same thing happened with the next four balls he threw. I couldn't resist teasing him.

"What's the matter, Aaron?" I laughed. "Out of practice?"

I spoke too soon.

With his last ball, he hit the bull's-eye and down I went into the water.

It was cold. Icy cold! I popped up and swam for the side as quickly as I could. Coach Morrison was waiting for me and handed me a towel to dry off my face. The rest of me, unfortunately, was dripping wet.

"Who's out of practice, Em?" Aaron called out.

"Come on, Emma," Michael said as he began juggling his baseballs. "Back upstairs.

It's my turn now."

I glowered at both my brothers as I climbed back up the ladder. How could they do this to me? Their baby sister! My outfit was ruined! Not to mention my shoes. My beautiful shoes! I'd hardly worn them this summer, wanting to save them for special occasions. Oh, they both owed me big-time!

I sat back down on the plank, sticking my tongue out at Michael.

"Ready?" he called out.

Before I could even answer, he'd thrown his first ball and I was back in the water.

The same thing happened when he threw his third ball.

And the fifth.

I was climbing back up the ladder for what I figured would be another dunking—Michael still had one more ball to throw—when Gwen came running up to me.

"Emma! I'm back!"

I was never so glad to see someone in my entire life!

"It's all yours," I said, my teeth chattering.

"You know what?" I heard Michael say to Aaron.

"What?"

"I'm tired of throwing baseballs. Why don't we go get something to eat?"

And with that they left the booth.

Ooooh! I was going to kill them when I got home tonight! Because if Gwen hadn't shown up, I knew for a fact that Michael would have thrown that last baseball. And I probably would have been dunked again!

"How bad do I look?" I asked Gwen.

"You want me to lie or do you want the truth?"

"The truth."

"Pretty bad."

I sighed. "Thanks."

"Actually, I don't think you look that bad," a voice said from behind me.

No.

It couldn't be.

He'd said he couldn't go to the fair.

That something suddenly came up.

But it *was* his voice, wasn't it?

Dreading what I was going to see, I turned around, in all my soaking-wet glory, and found myself facing Kyle.

Chapter Eleven

I wanted to disappear.

Immediately.

Why did I always look my absolute *worst* when I crossed paths with Kyle?

Why couldn't he have found me a few hours earlier when I was looking like a burst of sunshine? I'd have given Red a run for her money then!

Now I looked like I'd been caught in a hurricane. I'd lost an earring, my hair was a mess, and I squished when I walked. Kyle, on the other hand, in his khakis, blue-and-white striped polo shirt, baseball jacket, and dock-siders, looked like he'd stepped out of the pages of an Abercrombie & Fitch catalog.

"Kyle!" I tried to inject some warmth into my voice even though I was cold from all my dunkings and my teeth were starting to chatter. It had gotten a bit overcast and it wasn't as warm as it had been earlier. "W-w-what are you doing here? I thought something came up?"

I couldn't resist throwing his words back at him. At the same time, I wasn't going to play Twenty Questions with him.

But I was entitled to at least one question, wasn't I?

"My plans changed and your mom told me you went to the fair," he explained.

It was on the tip of my tongue to ask him about Red but I decided not to. It was none of my business.

But if Kyle was dating Red, then why was he here with me?

Did Red back out of plans that she had made with Kyle?

Was I his second choice?

Cathy's words bounced around my head: *Guys who two-time are jerks. Steer clear of them. Once a cheater, always a cheater.*

But it wasn't like Kyle and I were even dating. Hardly! We were just friends. Obviously, he must have wanted to spend the afternoon with me or he wouldn't have come to the fair. Right?

"You look like you could use a change of clothes," Gwen said. "Why don't we head in back for a little repair work?"

I quickly followed after Gwen.

"You're a lifesaver!" I told her once we were alone and I filled her in on Kyle.

"Don't thank me yet. You don't know what I'm giving you to wear."

"Anything's better than what I have on now," I said as I squeezed the sleeve of my shirt and water dripped to the floor.

Fifteen minutes later I was wearing a pair of gray sweatpants, a navy blue tank top, and a pair of flip-flops that Gwen had brought along in case she got dunked. My hair was somewhat dry and pulled back in a ponytail.

So I didn't look like a cover model.

I looked like the girl next door.

"Not the most fashionable things from my closet," Gwen apologized. "But at least they're dry." She held up my wet clothes and shoes. "I'll drop these off at your house later."

I gave her a hug. "Thanks for everything!"

"What are friends for?"

I rejoined Kyle at the front of the dunking booth.

"Are you still cold?" he asked.

Before I could answer, Kyle took off his baseball jacket and wrapped it around my shoulders. I slipped my arms into the sleeves. Even though the jacket was big, it was toasty warm!

"So what kind of girl are you when it comes to rides?" Kyle asked as we walked through the crowd.

"What kind of rides do you like?"

Kyle wagged a finger in my face. "No fair. I asked you first."

"I'm more of a merry-go-round type of girl. I don't like rides that flip you upside down or toss you from side to side."

A look of disappointment washed over Kyle's face. "You don't?"

Oh no! Suddenly I had realized my mistake. Why had I told him the truth? I should have told him I liked all kinds of rides and then waited to see what he said. Dumb, dumb, dumb!

"What kind of rides do you like?" I asked again, hoping to do some damage control.

He shrugged. "It doesn't matter."

"Tell me! Come on, you have to tell me. I told you!"

"I like crazy rides and I love roller coasters."

Gulp! I absolutely *hated* roller coasters.

Kyle looked at me, waiting for me to say something. Was he waiting for me to suggest we take a ride on the roller coaster? Sorry. Uh-uh. No way. *Not* going to happen. I know there are girls who'll pretend to be into things that the guys they like are into. But that's not me. Well . . . it's not me when it comes to roller coasters!

When Kyle realized I wasn't going to suggest we take a ride on the roller coaster, he looked even more glum.

We were passing by a concession stand that was making fresh lemonade. "I'm thirsty," Kyle said. "I'm going to get some lemonade."

I waited for Kyle to ask me if I wanted some too. But he didn't. Instead, he bought his lemonade and started drinking it through a straw. I waited for him to offer me a sip but he didn't.

"Mmm. This is good."

Really? I wanted to say. *How would I know unless you offered me a taste?*

I waited for Kyle to offer me his straw so I could take a sip, but he didn't. He just kept sipping and sipping as I watched the lemonade in his clear plastic cup disappear. Finally, realizing he wasn't going to offer me some, I reached into my pocket and put my money down on the counter. Actually, I *slammed* my coins down on the counter, I was so mad. Was he too cheap to buy me a lemonade?!

"One lemonade, please."

After getting my lemonade, I joined Kyle, who was sitting on a bench and crunching the ice cubes in his cup.

"What are the girls like at your school?" he asked.

I choked on the lemonade I was sipping and started coughing. *What kind of a question was that?!*

Kyle began pounding me on the back. "Hey! Are you okay?"

"Fine," I croaked out between coughs. "Just fine."

"You sure?"

I nodded. "What was that question again?"

"The girls at your school. What are they like? Are they friendly? Snooty?"

I wanted to scream, *"Why are you asking about other girls when you're here with me?!"* Instead, I asked, "What were the girls at your old school like?"

"They were okay but I knew most of them from when we started in kindergarten. There was nothing to figure out."

"Figure out?"

"I knew everything there was to know about them. Is it that way with the girls you go to school with?"

"Most, but not all. Some of them are hard to get to know."

"You mean they're mysterious?"

I shrugged. "I guess you could say that. Why?"

"I like it when a girl is mysterious."

"You do?" I said, trying not to sound bummed. I am so *not* mysterious. I was just Kyle's wacky next-door neighbor who always looked a mess.

Kyle nodded. "Yeah. A mystery keeps you guessing and it's almost like trying to put together a puzzle. You've got all the pieces but you don't know how they all fit together."

"Have you met a lot of mysterious girls?"

Kyle gave me a coy smile. "I have."

It was on the tip of my tongue to say, *"Like Ravishing Red?"*

But I didn't. Of course he meant Ravishing Red! She had probably intrigued him with her mysteriousness! Whatever that was! How mysterious could you be when you were a freshman in high school? I was just me. Emma

Miller. What you see is what you get. And if that wasn't good enough for Kyle, well, then I guess I didn't stand a chance with him. He wasn't acting like we were on a date. He was just hanging out with me.

But then Kyle surprised me, jumping off the bench we were sitting on and taking my hand in his. Holding it. What was going on?!

"Want to go on the Ferris wheel?" he asked.

The Ferris wheel was a ride I could handle. It was calm. Soothing. All we had to do was sit.

And Ferris wheels could be romantic!

"Yes!" I immediately answered.

As we walked over to the Ferris wheel— still holding hands!—Kyle bought a hot dog and slathered it with ketchup and mustard, eating it with both hands, much to my disappointment. No more hand-holding. Wah!

When we took our seats on the Ferris wheel, I noticed that Kyle had a smidge of ketchup on the corner of his mouth.

"You've got ketchup on your face," I said, pointing with a finger.

He wiped his mouth with a napkin. "Gone?"

I shook my head. "Still there."

He wiped again. "Gone now?"

"Here, let me," I said, reaching over to take the napkin out of his hand. As I did, the Ferris wheel started to move and I fell into Kyle's lap.

"Emma! I didn't know you liked me that much!"

I blushed as I scooted back over to my side of the seat.

Did Kyle know that I really liked him or was he just joking around?

"You don't have to sit so far away from me," Kyle said, pretending to pout.

I closed the distance between us and wiped at the ketchup on his mouth. "Better?"

He gave me a smile. "Much."

I smiled back, wondering, *Was Kyle flirting with me?* It sure seemed like he was. Did that mean he liked me, despite my lack of mysteriousness? Before I could explore that thought, though, I noticed something. The Ferris wheel had stopped moving.

I took a look around.

And saw we were almost at the very top!

"Why isn't the Ferris wheel moving?" I asked, trying to sound calm. "Why did it stop?"

I scooted closer to Kyle, who wrapped a reassuring arm around me.

"Don't be scared," he said.

"I'm not scared. Who says I'm scared?"

"We're only going to be at the top for a couple of minutes," he said. "Look, there's a shooting star. Quick, make a wish."

I followed Kyle's pointing finger, but I couldn't find the shooting star. Had there really been one or was Kyle trying to distract me?

Or . . .

Was it something else?

Was Kyle trying to be romantic? Did he maybe want to kiss me?

I had to admit, it was nice being so close to him. I felt safe with his arm around me. And he smelled just as good as I remembered.

I turned to face Kyle. We were nose to nose, our mouths only inches away from each other's.

Kiss me! I silently urged him. *Kiss me!*

Something must have been wrong with my transmission, because Kyle didn't kiss me. He

186

just kept looking at me.

Was he waiting for me to make the first move? To give him some sort of sign to let him know that I wanted him to kiss me?

But it was up to the guy to make the first move! Wasn't it?

"I must need glasses," I finally joked, turning my face away from his and looking up in the sky, "because I can't find it. I guess that means I don't get a wish."

But if I had gotten a wish, I would have wished for you to kiss me!

Just then the Ferris wheel started up again and we made our descent back to the ground.

My opportunity for a kiss was gone.

After we got off the Ferris wheel, I felt more confident with Kyle. He *had* to like me. With the exception of the Tunnel of Love, which our fair didn't have, the Ferris wheel was one of the most romantic rides around. And Kyle *did* ask me to sit close to him, he *did* put his arm around me, and he *did* pretend that there was a shooting star. He was sending me signals!

I decided I was going to take action.

We were walking through the fair again when I decided to slip my hand into his.

I expected him to take my hand and hold it.

Maybe swing it back and forth with his as we walked.

But he didn't.

Instead, he dropped it like a hot potato.

What was going on?!

I took a look around. Were Aaron and Michael headed our way? Was that why he'd let go? Why didn't he want to hold my hand? Before we'd gone on the Ferris wheel, he'd taken my hand in his. He'd held it while we walked until he'd bought his hot dog.

But now he didn't want to hold it?

"I'm going to buy a snow cone," Kyle said. "Be right back."

Hmmm. Was that why he had let go of my hand? Because he was going to buy a snow cone?

Of course he didn't ask me if I wanted one. Just like when he bought his lemonade and his hot dog. When you're on a date, the guy usually pays for the girl. But were we on a date? I didn't know! There were times when Kyle was acting like we *were* on a date (he *did* pay for my ticket for the Ferris wheel) and then there were times when he was acting like we *weren't*.

Could it be that Kyle was just clueless when it came to dating?

Or was he just cheap?!

"I liked meeting your friend the other day," he said when he rejoined me. I walked next to him, not having the confidence to take his hand back in mine. And *he* wasn't initiating any hand-holding either.

I gave him a puzzled look. "Caitlyn?" Why was he asking about Caitlyn?

"Yeah. She seemed nice."

"She's very nice. We've been best friends for years."

"She reminds me of someone I'm close to."

I'll just bet, I thought, instantly connecting the dots. Caitlyn was a redhead, and Ravishing Red was a redhead, too. Did Kyle have a thing for redheads? If he did, was I going to have to dye my hair red to get any sort of attention from him?

And if he *did* have a thing for redheads, did that mean I had to also be worrying about *Caitlyn* as well as Red?!

It was all too much to figure out. My head was hurting.

"What do you want to do next?" Kyle asked.

I sighed and gave him an honest answer. "I just want to go home."

Kissing Kyle was the last thing on my mind.

But another opportunity presented itself when we got home.

We'd gotten a ride home from the fair with Caitlyn and her older sister, Tess. I think Caitlyn was afraid to be alone with Tess and that's why she asked us if we wanted a ride. As I'd suspected, Caitlyn had borrowed Tess's high heels without asking. Not only that, but she'd broken one of the heels. Caitlyn was in *major* hot water. To make matters worse, she hadn't had any luck finding Aaron at the fair even though I had kept running into him.

"If I'm still alive tomorrow, I'll come by in

the afternoon," Caitlyn whispered to me as Tess dropped us off. "You can tell me all about your day with Kyle. And maybe even your good-night kiss!"

"Shhh!" I hissed, hoping Kyle hadn't heard her. He was far away enough from the curb that I didn't think so.

After Tess and Caitlyn drove off, I walked with Kyle to my front lawn.

"I had a really nice time today," I told him.

Well, it hadn't been a *really* nice time but there had been some nice moments.

"Me too," Kyle said.

And then there was an awkward silence.

I smiled at Kyle and he smiled back but neither one of us said anything.

Okay, this is it! Your cue to show me that you really did have a nice time today. You have to kiss me. Kiss me!

This time it did seem like Kyle was able to read my mind. He moved closer to me and put a hand on my shoulder. All the doubts that had been running through my mind at the fair were gone. He *did* like me and he was going to show me with a kiss!

But then my long-awaited kiss didn't happen.

Just as I moved closer to Kyle, hoping against hope that I was finally going to get my first kiss, the front door to my house opened up and Aaron screamed, "HEY, EM! WHAT'S TAKING YOU SO LONG TO COME INSIDE? MOM AND DAD WANT TO LOCK UP THE HOUSE AND GO TO SLEEP!"

At the sound of Aaron's voice, Kyle took a step back from me.

The moment was gone.

Had he been planning to kiss me? If he had, I'd never know.

"I should be getting home," Kyle said, pointing a thumb over his shoulder. "I've got a curfew."

I nodded. "Okay."

"Talk to you later?"

"You know where to find me," I said, trying not to feel (or sound!) disappointed that once again I hadn't been kissed.

Kyle nodded back. "Good night."

"Night," I said, walking to my front door and waving good-bye.

After I got up to my bedroom, I realized I was still wearing Kyle's baseball jacket. Even though a part of me wished I could keep it, I knew I'd have to return it to him tomorrow.

But for tonight I could pretend that Kyle was my boyfriend and that he had given me his baseball jacket to wear because he wanted everyone to know I was his girl.

I slipped my hands into the jacket's pockets and whirled around in front of my bedroom mirror.

As my hands slipped into the pockets, a folded piece of paper fell out, along with some ticket stubs, grocery store receipts, and chewing gum wrappers. Picking up the folded piece of paper, I saw it was a printout from a website.

As I took a closer look at the page, my mouth dropped open.

It was an email from Dear Daisy to Romeo.

What would Kyle be doing with an email from Daisy?

And why would he have an email that Romeo had sent?

Unless . . .

No.

It couldn't be.

It just couldn't be!

I sat down on my bed in shock. I wanted to deny it, but I couldn't. Not when I was holding the proof in my hands.

Kyle was Romeo?!

Chapter Twelve XOXOX

Kyle was Romeo.

Like a big neon sign, the words kept flashing in my mind: *KYLE IS ROMEO. KYLE IS ROMEO. KYLE IS ROMEO.*

I didn't want to believe it, but it was true.

Absolutely, positively.

There was no denying it.

The proof was in my hands.

And that proof was the email that I had sent Romeo last night.

The email where I told him to go after the girl he liked.

Words I had written hours ago jumped out at me: *you're still into this girl . . . go after her . . . give her another chance.*

I groaned and crumpled the email into a ball, throwing it across my bedroom as I finally realized what had happened. Kyle had been writing to Daisy for advice about a girl he liked. It certainly hadn't been *me* he'd been writing about because I sounded *nothing* like the girl he'd described in his emails. And tonight he had told me what kind of girl he liked. A girl who was *mysterious*. Again, *not* me.

Ravishing Red was the girl who had Kyle's heart. I'd seen it for myself this morning with my own eyes. The two of them had looked *very* cozy together and I had told Kyle to go after her. To give her another chance.

Which he'd done.

The guy *I* liked had been writing to me about a girl *he* liked and I told him what he needed to do to get her.

Oh, I was such an idiot!

Even though there was no way I could have known that Kyle was Romeo, why hadn't I been up front with him from the beginning and just told him how I felt? Why didn't I follow my own advice? I was always telling my girlfriends that if they liked a guy, they should just tell him. But I hadn't done that with Kyle.

Maybe if I had I would have had a chance.

Maybe he would have lost interest in Ravishing Red and started thinking of me as girlfriend material.

Now it was all over.

I had lost whatever chance I had with him.

I couldn't share my feelings with him. Couldn't tell him that I liked him. Not when I knew he liked someone else. That would be too humiliating. I could just see the look in his eyes. He'd squirm and be uncomfortable and then he'd tell me, "That's nice, Emma. But I don't like you the way you like me. I like someone else."

I threw myself down on my bed and buried my face in a pillow. I could feel tears at the corners of my eyes but I was *not* going to cry. This wasn't the end of the world. I could have had something with Kyle and I blew it.

I didn't have anyone to blame but myself.

I barely slept a wink that night. When I wasn't tossing and turning in my bed, I was having nightmares. In one dream Kyle and Ravishing Red were getting married in a church and I was one of the bridesmaids. When the minister asked if anyone objected to the two of them getting married, I wanted to scream and tell Kyle not to marry her, but I had no voice. In another dream Kyle and Red were filthy rich and eating in a restaurant where I was the waitress who had to serve them. Red was wearing furs and jewels and looking like a cover model while I was dressed in a potato sack and my hair was a mess of split ends.

In the middle of each dream I would always wake up, my heart pounding furiously. Eventually I would realize that I was home in my bed and that it had all been a dream. With a sigh of relief, I would then close my eyes and another horrible dream would unfold.

When morning finally arrived, I decided the first thing I was going to do was return Kyle's baseball jacket. Before finding Kyle's Romeo email, I had been thinking of keeping the jacket and making up some sort of excuse as to why I couldn't find it. Now I just wanted it gone. It was too much of a painful reminder of what could have been. Maybe not having the jacket around would help me get over Kyle.

Phase two of my plan was to avoid Kyle for the rest of the summer. That wouldn't be too hard. I would just spend as much time as possible over at Caitlyn's. Hopefully by the time classes started in September, whatever feelings I'd had for Kyle would be gone and seeing him around wouldn't hurt as much.

Of course, I'd have to deal with seeing him with Ravishing Red but I'd worry about that later.

Today I had his jacket to return.

The last thing I wanted to do was run into him so I'd have to time things carefully. I positioned myself in my bedroom, pressed against the side of my window where I had been the day before when I'd been spying on Kyle and Ravishing Red. After an hour I finally got lucky when Kyle's father left the house with

Megan, followed a few minutes later by Kyle and Tommy. I'd bet money that Tommy *loved* Ravishing Red. Why wouldn't he? She wasn't me!

Once the coast was clear I grabbed Kyle's jacket and headed next door. I knew Mrs. O'Reilly was still home because her car was in the driveway. I knocked on the back door and waited for her to answer. When no one came to the door, I knocked again. Finally, I knocked a third time and then tried the door. It was open.

I walked inside and called out, "Hello? Anyone home?"

I could hear the sound of the washing machine coming from the basement. I walked to the door at the end of the kitchen and stuck my head in. "Hello! Mrs. O'Reilly?"

She turned from a pile of laundry she was sorting through and gave me a smile. "Hi, Emma!"

I held up Kyle's baseball jacket. "Kyle lent me this last night. I wanted to return it."

"You can just toss it in his bedroom. It's

upstairs at the end of the hall."

After leaving Mrs. O'Reilly, I headed upstairs and found Kyle's bedroom. I don't know what I was expecting but Kyle's bedroom was no different than my brothers'. Clothes were tossed everywhere. There were piles of DVDs and CDs on the floor. Magazines and newspapers and messy piles of paper were scattered across his desk. There was a computer in one corner and a TV in the other.

I tossed Kyle's jacket on his unmade bed, wanting to get out of his house as quickly as possible. As I headed out of the room, I noticed a sketchbook on the top of his desk. Remembering how he said he wanted to be a cartoonist, I couldn't resist taking a peek. What could it hurt?

As I flipped through the pages of the sketchbook, my mouth dropped open.

I couldn't believe what I was seeing.

Was it possible to be shocked two days in a row?

The sketches in the book were caricatures.

The first sketch was called "The Girl with the Clay Face" and it was the image of a girl with a huge mudpack on her face.

The second sketch was "The Dust Diva," followed by "The Thing That Came to Shop."

A fourth sketch, which wasn't finished yet, was called "Aqua Girl" and it showed a girl in all her soaking-wet glory at a county fair.

Clearly, the girl in every sketch was *me*.

And in every sketch, Kyle had captured me at my absolute *worst*!

I was angry.

Very angry.

Who did Kyle think he was, making fun of me this way?

I flipped through a few more pages but they were blank. Naturally there were no caricatures of Ravishing Red. Of course not. She was Miss Perfect. Miss Mysterious. She wasn't a walking joke who provided Kyle with hours of sketching material. Not like me, Miss Wacky Neighbor!

At that moment all I wanted to do was rip

each and every page out of his sketchbook and rip them into teeny-tiny shreds. But I couldn't do that.

Instead I threw the sketchbook back down on Kyle's desk and stormed out of his bedroom.

Chapter Thirteen

I was so angry, I felt like steam was coming out of my ears.

I wanted to scream.

How could Kyle do this to me? I thought he was a nice guy, but obviously he wasn't. He saw me as nothing more than a joke!

I stomped downstairs and hurried through the kitchen, wanting to get as far away from his house as possible. But my progress was halted when I stormed out the back door and found myself crashing into a wall of solid muscle.

Correction.

A wall of solid *crunchy* muscle.

Kyle and I stood face-to-face, our bodies pressed together.

Between us was a sopping-wet bag of groceries filled with a dozen broken eggs.

We were both a gooey, eggy mess.

I pulled away from Kyle and saw that my tank top was all wet from the smashed eggs. So was his.

"Hey!" Tommy shouted, popping out from behind Kyle. "She broke our eggs!"

Kyle stared at me without saying anything and then he started laughing. "I guess she was so *egg*-cited to see us, she couldn't stop running."

It's very rare that I lose my temper. Even with Rob, Michael, and Aaron constantly driving me crazy, I never lose it.

But Kyle's laughter pushed me over the edge and I exploded.

"You think this is funny? You think I'm a joke?" I shouted. "Are you going to draw a sketch of me all covered with eggs and call it 'Ms. Eggcentric'? I bet you haven't been drawing caricatures of your mystery girl, have you?"

Kyle, stunned at my anger, stopped laughing and stared at me in confusion. "Mystery girl? What mystery girl?"

His question only made me angrier. How dumb did he think I was?

"*This* mystery girl!" I announced, waving the email I had found in his jacket. I should have thrown it out but instead I'd been carrying it around since this morning, picking it up off my bedroom floor from where I'd thrown it the night before. I must have reread it at least fifty times, each time hating myself for telling Kyle to give Ravishing Red another chance. "Don't try and deny it. I know all about her because you've been writing to Dear Daisy." To prove it, I began quoting from some of Kyle's other emails.

A look of panic crossed Kyle's face as my words sunk in.

Aha! Caught!

Kyle snatched the piece of paper out of my hand. "How do you know I've been writing to Daisy? Who told you?" He gasped.

"Did she tell you?"

I knew I was supposed to keep it a secret. I knew I wasn't supposed to tell anyone. But I couldn't help myself. I wanted to shock him. Big-time.

"No one had to tell me."

"Then how do you know?" He waved the email in my face. "How?"

"I know because *I'm* Daisy!" I announced smugly.

Tommy tugged on the bottom of Kyle's tank top. "I thought her name was Emma," he said. "How come she doesn't know her name is Emma? Is she crazy? She looks crazy," he said, staring at me warily as he edged himself behind his big brother.

That's right, I'm crazy. Crazy for your brother and look where it's gotten me. All covered with eggs and ranting like a crazy girl on your back porch. I'm surprised the neighbors aren't watching. A real live soap opera. With no commercial interruptions!

"*You're* Daisy?" Kyle whispered, looking first at me and then at the email he was holding.

Then back at me and back at the email.

"Uh-huh. And if I'd known it was you who was asking for advice, I never would have given it!"

"How come?" he asked. "I thought Daisy was supposed to help the people who wrote to her. Why wouldn't you want to help me?"

The words were on the tip of my tongue. *Because I like you,* I wanted to say. *I like you so much but you don't like me. You like someone else.* But I couldn't get the words out. I couldn't allow myself to be humiliated any more than I already was.

So instead of answering I turned my back on Kyle and ran across our yards and into my house without looking back.

Chapter Fourteen

Nothing hurts more than a broken heart. There's no way to really describe the pain. It's not a physical pain. I've experienced that. I've skinned my knees and elbows while Rollerblading more times than I can count. When I was seven I broke my arm when I crashed into an apple tree (Aaron and I were racing our bikes). I've fallen on my chin and bitten my tongue while ice-skating. When those things happened, I was *instantly* in pain. The pain was sharp. Jabbing. *Excruciating.* I screamed. I cried. But eventually the pain went away and I felt better.

But this was different.

It was like a dull ache throughout my entire body.

And it didn't go away immediately.

Almost like it's reminding you of what you've lost.

And I'd lost Kyle.

As a friend and as a possible boyfriend.

I wondered how long I was going to feel this way because I was *not* liking it. It had been hours since my confrontation with Kyle and I was still a jumble of emotions. If only I could turn back the clock and be honest with him. Tell him how I really felt. Maybe things would be different.

I couldn't stop thinking of Ravishing Red. I was *so* jealous of her. Because she had Kyle. If only I'd told him my feelings, I might have had a chance with him. *Why* hadn't I followed my own advice? What had I been afraid of? What was the worst thing that could have happened? Kyle would have said he didn't feel the same way about me. That would have been it. I would have felt lousy for a day or two, a week tops, but then I would have moved on. Now I'd always be wondering:

What if?

What if?

What if?

What if I'd told him how I really felt?

But it was too late.

What's done is done.

Caitlyn stopped by the house after dinner with a pint of strawberry ice cream, my favorite. She'd called me that afternoon to tell me what had happened with her sister, Tess (they had a *major* fight, with Tess calling Caitlyn a thief and demanding she pay for the shoe she'd broken. Caitlyn's parents backed up Tess and now Caitlyn had to cough up the cash). As soon as I said hello she could hear something was wrong and began asking me questions. I told her that everything was fine and got off the phone as quickly as I could. I was afraid if I stayed on I would crack and tell her everything. Obviously I hadn't convinced her.

"Tell me what's wrong," she insisted, handing

me the pint of ice cream while she rummaged through our refrigerator for whipped cream and chocolate syrup. She found the ice-cream scooper in a drawer and took two bowls out of the cabinet over the stove.

"Fill me in," she said as she began scooping out ice cream.

Thinking it might help to tell her the entire story, I started from the beginning, confessing about being Daisy and ending with how I had sabotaged myself with Kyle.

"Oh, sweetie," Caitlyn said, forgetting all about the ice-cream sundaes she'd been making and giving me a huge hug. "I'm so sorry! Is there anything I can do?"

Before I could respond, Aaron sauntered into the kitchen and began helping himself to the ice cream that Caitlyn had brought for me. Without even asking!

"That's *my* ice cream," I said, snatching a bowl away from him. "Caitlyn brought it over to cheer me up."

"Why? What's wrong?"

"Hi, Aaron," Caitlyn said in the flirty voice

she uses whenever she's around a guy she likes.

"Hey, Caitlyn."

I had to say, my brother looked good for a change. He was wearing a sleeveless black T-shirt, which showed off his muscular arms, and a new pair of jeans. He must have just taken a shower, because he looked clean for once. "Where are you going all dressed up?" I asked.

"My friend Ryan is having a party. He said some cute girls might be there."

There was no mistaking the hurt look that washed over Caitlyn's face when she heard those words. I wanted to scream at her: *If you don't want to lose him to someone else, tell him you like him!*

What happened next left me speechless. It was like Caitlyn had read my mind seconds earlier.

"Aaron, I have to tell you something," she said.

"What?" he asked, holding the can of whipped cream over his mouth and giving himself a big squirt. So big that it spilled over the sides of his mouth. Ugh! *So* juvenile.

"I like you," she announced. "And I want to go out with you. I know you probably think of me as another bratty sister, but I'm not. I think you're really, really cute. So, what do you think about that?"

I looked at my brother and I had an expression on my face that warned him he'd better think *very* carefully about what he said. Not that it would have made any difference. Aaron answers to no one, but *no one* hurts my best friend!

For a second he just stood still. Then he shrugged, licking whipped cream off the sides of his mouth with his tongue. "I'd be up for a movie. Maybe grab a burger afterward?"

Caitlyn's mouth dropped open and she looked stunned. I have to admit, I felt pretty stunned myself. I hadn't expected Aaron to say what he did.

"Does that sound good?" he asked.

Caitlyn found her voice. "Sure."

"How about tonight? I really didn't want to go to Ryan's party anyway. Got any plans?"

"No!" she answered right away.

"Let me go online and see what's playing at the multiplex."

After he left, I asked Caitlyn, "What just happened here?"

"Your brother asked me out on a date!"

"Duh! I know that. But what made you decide to confess how you felt?"

"It was you."

"Me?"

"Yeah. If you'd told Kyle the way you felt, maybe you would have had a chance with him."

I put my head down on the kitchen table and moaned, "I know. I know. Don't remind me."

"I know this sounds mean and horrible and selfish and I don't mean it to. But I didn't want what happened to you to happen to me so I decided to be honest with Aaron. You scared me straight! Actually, it's what you've been telling me to do all along. I just didn't have the courage to do it until I saw how miserable you were."

I lifted my head off the table. "And it's

my own fault. Well, I'm glad something good came out of my stupidity."

"You're not stupid!"

"Yes, I am. Here I am giving advice to everyone else about their love life and I make a mess out of mine! I shouldn't even be writing a column. What do I know about love?" I didn't wait for Caitlyn to answer. "Nothing!"

"Don't be so hard on yourself," Caitlyn said, giving me a hug. "Sometimes it's easier to figure things out for other people instead of yourself. You really are good at this advice stuff!"

If only I was!

After Caitlyn and Aaron left for the movies (Caitlyn decided they should go see a horror movie. "That way I can wrap my arm around his and bury my face in his shoulder during the scary parts!" she confided to me), I went up to my room and turned on my computer. I was trying very hard not to feel sorry for myself. If only I'd done what Caitlyn had done with Aaron. Maybe I wouldn't be home alone. Maybe I'd be with someone special.

I don't know why I did it, but I decided to check Daisy's email account. When I did, I found an email waiting from Romeo.

It had been sent that afternoon.

At first I wanted to delete it. What could Kyle possibly have to say to me? And how much more pain did I want to subject myself to?

And if he *did* have something to say to me, why hadn't he just picked up the phone? Or better yet, just knocked on my door?

It did make sense, though. After all, this whole mess had started online. Why not finish it the same way?

I hesitated before clicking the email open. I should just delete it. But part of me wanted to read it. I was curious.

So I opened it up.

Dear Daisy: Remember that crazy girl I told you about? Well, I still like her. I really like her. Any advice?

Advice?! He wanted advice from me about

217

Ravishing Red? Hadn't I been tortured enough? Was this his idea of some sick joke?

Red had won!

Game over!

To the victor belong the spoils!

Or did Red have so many guys to choose from that Kyle felt he didn't have a chance with her? Was he feeling insecure? Was that what this was all about? Was I supposed to be his "coach" and stroke his ego so he'd feel good about himself and confident enough to go after Red?

I angrily deleted the email. He could figure things out with Red on his own!

But no sooner had I deleted his email then another one arrived seconds later. Like the first email, I couldn't just delete it. I wanted to, but at the same time, I wanted to know what he had to say. Because this time I was going to answer him back.

Dear Daisy: I really need your advice. This girl that I like thinks that I like someone else but there is no Mystery Girl. The girl I like is the girl next door.

My mouth dropped open as I reread the words on the screen in front of me.

The girl I like is the girl next door.

I was the girl next door.
What?
Wait. Wait.
Kyle liked me??
ME!!!

Chapter Fifteen

Even though the words were right in front of me, I still couldn't believe it.

Kyle liked me.

HE LIKED ME!!!

But how could that be? What about Ravishing Red?

I knew I had to respond to Kyle's email, but I didn't know what to say. Should I admit that I liked him too? I was just getting ready to start typing when the doorbell rang, breaking my concentration. Rats!

Then the doorbell rang again.

And again.

"Will someone please answer the door?" I called out, trying to sound sweet and not bossy. "I'm in the middle of doing something very important."

My fingers hovered over my keyboard. What was I supposed to write back? I almost felt like I was being given a second chance with Kyle. I didn't want to mess things up!

Before I could start typing, the doorbell rang again, only this time the ring was drawn out. Like the person ringing the doorbell was keeping their finger on the bell for a really long time.

Argh! I wanted to ignore the ringing, but I couldn't. It was driving me crazy. And I wanted to write back to Kyle. The sooner the better. If he was still online, I wanted him to get my email tonight and write back ASAP!

The only way I'd be able to send this email was to get rid of whoever was at the front door. Obviously Rob and Michael, who I knew were both home, weren't going to answer the door. And my parents were both out. So if I wanted the ringing to stop, I'd have to go answer the door.

I left my computer and stormed out of my bedroom, stomping downstairs. Who could it be? And what was so important that they had to keep ringing our bell? Why didn't they just leave and come back another time?

I flung open the front door. "What?!" I demanded impatiently. "What do you want?!"

The person on the other side of the door took a step back.

It was Kyle.

Oops!

"Kyle!" I exclaimed with a smile, trying to do major damage control. *Why* did he always get to see me at my *worst*?! "What a surprise! I didn't know it was you ringing the bell."

"Are you sure?" he asked somewhat warily.

"I swear!" I said, trying not to sound panicked, crossing my heart, and hoping he wouldn't leave, that I hadn't scared him off!

He took a step closer. "I hope I wasn't bothering you."

I shook my head. "You weren't. I was online. Answering emails. But I didn't know what to say," I admitted. "Sometimes it's hard to find the right words."

Kyle nodded in understanding. "I know. But how about if I say something? Or rather, show you something?"

"Show me something?" I asked, puzzled. "Show me what?"

"This," Kyle said, opening up his sketch-book.

"I already saw those," I said as Kyle flipped to the pages with the caricatures I'd seen that morning. I did *not* want to see them again. I felt embarrassed. They showed me at my all-time worst. Girls, want to know how to scare a guy away? Just flip through Kyle's sketchbook to see how Emma does it.

"But you didn't see everything," he explained.

As Kyle turned to the back pages of his sketchbook, I could see there were more caricatures that I hadn't seen. Of his mother. Of Tommy and Megan. Even my own brothers! And they were all hysterically funny. If I'd bothered flipping through the rest of his sketchbook I would have seen them, but I'd been so angry, I'd thrown down the book after seeing the way I'd been portrayed and stormed out.

Kyle closed his sketchbook. "I wasn't making fun of you," he explained. "I'm working on a comic book of my own. It's going to focus around a girl who has superpowers but has to constantly disguise herself in silly ways. That's why I did the caricatures. I do this with everybody."

"So you weren't making fun of me?"

Kyle shook his head. "How could I make fun of you, Emma? I think you're great."

"You do?"

HE THOUGHT I WAS GREAT!!!

"But I thought you didn't like me!" I blurted out before I could stop myself.

"Why would you think that?"

Where to begin?!

"Let's see," I said, counting off on my fingers. "After I took back Rob's comic books, you avoided me for days. You invited me to go with you to the fair and then you broke our date although it wasn't *officially* a date. When we were at the fair, you wouldn't hold my hand. You didn't buy me a lemonade *or* a snow cone. You asked me about *other* girls and told me that you liked girls who were mysterious." I held up eight fingers. "I could go on but I'm running out of fingers. Can you say 'mixed signals'? You were acting weird!" I then held up another finger. "And you never kissed me when you had the chance. And you had more than one chance!"

Kyle blushed. "I was only following Daisy's advice. When we were at the fair, instead of acting like myself, I kept trying to figure out what Daisy would do. I was always second-guessing myself. First, I'd think I should pretend I didn't like you. Then I'd think I *should* show you that I like you. The only reason I was writing to Daisy was because I could never figure you out! You were so mysterious!"

Suddenly, I felt like a computer that was on overload. I was processing too much information way too fast.

At the fair, Kyle had told me he liked girls who were mysterious.

And he just said that he thought *I* was mysterious.

He had also been writing to Daisy for advice about a girl he liked and following her advice.

And *I* was Daisy.

Which meant . . .

Which meant that Kyle had been writing to Daisy about *me*!

I was the girl he had liked all along!

And *I* had been giving him advice on how to deal with *me*!

I'd been sabotaging myself!

I began laughing hysterically.

"Are you okay?" Kyle asked.

"I'm fine," I giggled. "Really. You like me?"

Kyle nodded. "I can prove how much I like you," he said.

"You can? How?" Not that I needed more proof. He was telling me he liked me!

"I don't just do caricatures. I also do portraits."

Kyle opened up his sketchbook, flipped through the pages, and found what he was searching for. He turned the sketchbook around. "See?"

The portrait of me was breathtaking. It was so real. So lifelike. It was almost like looking into a mirror.

"Wow, I didn't know you could draw this well," I whispered in awe, staring at the image of myself. "It's beautiful."

"Guess you don't know everything about me."

I shook my head. "I guess I don't."

Kyle closed his sketchbook again and tucked it under his arm. "So you were in the middle of answering emails. Was one of them from Romeo?"

I nodded shyly. "So you really like the girl next door?"

"Uh-huh."

"That's me, right?"

Kyle laughed. "Right."

I couldn't help myself from asking the question. I had to know. After all, she was my competition. I had to know how Kyle felt about her. Was she his first choice or was I? How did I stand against her?

"So who's Red?"

"Red?"

"The gorgeous redhead I saw you with yesterday."

Now Kyle started laughing hysterically, clutching his sides.

"What's so funny?"

"That's my cousin Jessica! Her family was driving through town yesterday and they stopped by for a visit. That's why I had to cancel our plans. I wasn't sure how long Jessica was going to be around. But once she left, I was able to go to the fair and find you."

Ravishing Red was his cousin! She *wasn't* his girlfriend.

And he hadn't been writing to Daisy about her.

It had *always* been me!

D'oh!

I was supposed to be an advice expert and yet I'd made a mess of everything. I should have followed my own advice and told Kyle how I felt about him. Instead I'd been torturing myself for days! In that moment, I realized something. Maybe I wasn't cut out to be Dear Daisy. Or maybe, when it came to *my* love life, I needed a Dear Daisy of my own. Because when it came to love, I really didn't know as much as I thought I did. At least when it came to myself.

Kyle took my hand in his and gazed at it, slowly rubbing a thumb over my fingers. "You know, there was something else I wanted to ask Daisy."

"What?"

"How do you know when it's the right time to kiss a girl you like?"

"That's easy. You just do it."

Kyle looked at me shyly. "You do?"

"Yep," I said, my heart beating rapidly.

"Like this?" Kyle asked.

And with those words Kyle moved closer to me, leaned in, and kissed me.

Suddenly the whole world ceased to exist. It was just me and Kyle as his lips softly pressed against mine. Tingles traveled through-out my entire body and as Kyle kissed me, I couldn't help but kiss him back.

It was everything I had ever imagined it would be.

No, wait. Let me correct that.

It was better!

"Has anyone ever told you that you're an excellent kisser?" I said.

Kyle blushed. "Actually, no. I haven't had a lot of practice."

"Well, you know what they say."

"What?"

"Practice makes perfect."

Kyle nodded. "You're right."

And with those words, Kyle kissed me again.

I'm happy to say that his second kiss was just as excellent as his first.

Acknowledgments

Once again, I have a bunch of people to thank.

First, my editor, Lexa Hillyer, who lets me do what I love—write novels!—and then makes my novels better! I'm really lucky to have you as my editor.

To my agent, Evan Marshall, one of the best guys in publishing.

Jennifer Fisher, one of my best friends, who always puts a smile on my face when she gives me the latest updates on her daughter, Emma, and her son, Ben. I wish you were still living in New York!

My brother, Vincent, who used to listen to my stories when we were kids and would always ask for more.

And all my friends and coworkers who are always there for me and always willing to listen: David Korabik, Kevin O'Brien, Colleen Martin, Rosanna Aponte, Jim Pascale, Michael Thomas Ford, Elise Donner Smith, Tracy Bernstein, Beth Lieberman, Paul Dinas, Barbara Bennett, Neven Gravett, Susan Lisa Jackson, John Masiello, and Lou Malcangi.

If I've left anyone out, I'm sorry. I didn't mean to!

Ready for your next first kiss?
Here's an excerpt from
Trust Me
by Rachel Hawthorne

W e headed out the door. Towering oak trees circled the encampment. I could smell the scent of dirt and dampness and vegetation—nature as a whole. Several wooden cabins made up the camp. The main building was where registration took place. The nurse's station was also located inside. Then a couple of cabins where the campers were housed had been built nearby. A lead counselor slept in each cabin, to be on hand for emergencies or homesickness and to keep campers indoors after lights-out.

Liz and I were Counselors-in-Training. Otherwise known as CITs. We'd live in the dormitory with other CITs. Which was fine with me. I didn't particularly want to look after a dozen kids through the night. I was hoping to spend some of the evening looking after my love life.

1

Speaking of . . .

I pulled my cell phone out of my shorts pocket. Its display was flashing, NO SIGNAL.

"Still no luck?" Liz asked.

"Nope. I wonder why we never realized that cell phones couldn't get a signal out here," I stated.

"Maybe because we never had cell phones before."

We'd both recently turned fourteen, me two weeks before Liz. We'd both asked for the same thing for our birthday. Cell phones. Big surprise. Having the ability to constantly keep in touch with our friends was such a must. Text messaging was also the absolute best, and we had the code down long before we could put it to use.

I'd had visions of text messaging a guy counselor, "U R 2 CUTE." *Yeah, right, like I'd ever be that bold.*

My vast experience at communicating with guys mostly involved my brother, who was six years younger than me. Our conversations usually began with him whining, "I'm gonna tell Mom."

And my witty response: "Whatever."

I needed to seriously develop my flirtation skills—like figuring out what guys found interesting and what they wanted to talk about—and my brother was so not good practice material.

"Maybe once we go hiking, get farther away from camp, I'll be able to pick up a signal," I suggested hopefully, although I was beginning to suspect that the camp had been built in the one place that the Verizon-can-you-hear-me-now? guy had yet to visit.

Liz shook her head. "We're in the middle of nowhere. We should have expected this."

Or as my dad said, we were "on the *far*side of nowhere," which he seemed to think was worse than being in the middle of nowhere. I sorta figured nowhere was nowhere and it didn't have map coordinates. You were just there. No where.

"I think I'm going into cell phone withdrawal," I said, only half jokingly. My dad had constantly teased me for the last couple months that my hand was permanently curled in cell-phone-holding position. Of course, he said

Mom's hand was permanently curled in credit-card-holding position.

"I'm already there," Liz said. Her phone wasn't getting a signal either.

Even though Liz was the person I called most, and we would be side by side most of the summer, we'd planned to use our phones for communicating on the sly.

QT 2 R = *Cutie to the right.*

QT 2 L = *Cutie to the left.*

I angled the phone and snapped a picture of Liz. At least the camera still worked. My dad was all about gadgets. No way was he going to get me a plain old cell phone for my birthday. Like my dad, I saw the value in multifunctional products. I intended to take lots of pictures, so bringing the cell phone along wasn't a total waste.

As Liz and I approached the main office building, we spotted a group of people milling around in front. Judging by their uniforms, they were all CITs. None were the counselors from last year, although I did recognize some people who had been campers during previous summers. I guess everyone had the idea of moving up to better things.

"I wonder where Cute Casey is," Liz whispered.

I shrugged. "He's already trained. Maybe this week it's just the newbies."

"Right." She scowled.

I watched her freckles scrunch up. With red hair comes freckles. When we were a lot younger—and really bored—we would use a Sharpie to connect the freckles on her arms to create pictures. So whenever I looked at her cheek really closely now, I always saw a kite that I'd drawn by connecting freckles. Actually, kites were pretty much all I'd ever seen and drawn. It's fairly easy to see a kite in freckles. Does that make me unimaginative?

I didn't want to contemplate that it might, since being a counselor meant coming up with creative ways to keep the campers occupied and away from the boredom zone.

"But if the older counselors aren't here, who's going to train us?" Liz asked me. Obviously her scowl had represented her thinking face.

"I'm sure someone will."

"Hey!" A couple of girls had turned, noticed us, and hurried over. We'd met them last summer. Caryn and Torie — Victoria, according to the name embroidered on her shirt. They'd shared a cabin with us and participated in our makeover session.

We didn't have much time to catch up on the exciting things we'd done since last summer — which was fine with me, since I'd done very little that I would classify as exciting. Now that I was actually here, I was beginning to have doubts that I could be an amazing counselor. Could I lead? Could I keep the campers entertained? Could I protect and serve . . . oh, wait, that was the job of the police. Could I care for and console those who got homesick?

I was pretty sure I could, but soon I'd be tested.

Liz, Caryn, Torie, and I teased each other about the fact that none of us had kept our promise to stay in touch through e-mail or instant messaging. School has a way of taking up your time.

"I don't remember the counselors wearing these uniforms," Liz said. She was still hung up on not being entirely fashionable. Although trekking through the woods has a fashion of its own.

"Last year it was T-shirts," Caryn said. "I guess they wanted something a little classier."

"Classier?" Liz asked. "You think this is classier?"

"No, but I guess they thought it looked better than T-shirts."

"Maybe we'll get T-shirts after we finish this week of training," Torie said. "You know what I'm saying?"

"I liked T-shirts on the guy counselors," I admitted.

"Especially on Cute Casey," Liz said. "Anyone know if he's going to be here this year?"

Before anyone could answer, a clanging began. An iron triangle hung off the porch of the main lodge. Whenever our attention was needed, someone banged its insides with an iron rod. Our adventure camp had a rustic feel to it. While we had electricity, the bulbs always seemed to burn dimly. The TV in the dining hall, where we all gathered if we wanted to watch any television shows, was a very small screen and not high-def. The reception was lousy. No satellite dish. It did have a VHS tape player, but it wasn't exactly modern.

A woman—the tallest woman I'd ever seen, and her blond hair was practically buzzed—stood on the porch beside a man whose long dark hair was held in place with a leather tie. Excitement hummed on the air. In front of them stood four counselors I recognized from last year. Unfortunately, there wasn't a Casey, Hank, or George among them. I wondered what happened to those guys. They'd probably been the oldest of the crew, and it seemed like they'd been around forever. Surely they hadn't moved on to other things. Like college or the army or a real job.

Everyone who'd been standing around—talking and waiting for the meeting to begin—shuffled closer, jockeying for a better view. And that's when I noticed him.

Sean Reed.

"Oh, my gosh," Liz whispered harshly beside me. "Do you see—"

"I see."

"How are they even letting *him* be a CIT?" she asked. "That is so not fair!"

As usual, she was totally reading my mind.